Things I Cannot Say

INCENDIARY
Collection

Homage to
Beatriz Guido

Elssie Cano

THINGS I CANNOT SAY

Nueva York Poetry Press®

Nueva York Poetry Press LLC
128 Madison Avenue, Oficina 2NR
New York, NY 10016, USA
Teléfono: +1(929)354-7778
nuevayork.poetrypress@gmail.com
www.nuevayorkpoetrypress.com

Things I Cannot Say
©2023, Elssie Cano

ISBN-13: 978-1-958001-23-3

© Incendiary Collection vol. 2
(Homage to Beatriz Guido)

© Publisher:
Marisa Russo

© Editor:
Fred Acoleo

© Proofreader:
Edgar Smith

© Graphic Designer:
William Velásquez Vásquez

© Layout Designer
Francisco Trejo

© Photographers:
Hector Gutierrez Machorro

Cano, Elssie
Things I Cannot Say / Elssie Cano. 1ª ed. New York: Nueva York Poetry Press, 2023,
376 pp. 5.25" x 8".

1. Latin American Literature

For my children,
Giselle Massaro and John Cano.

How difficult to try to get out of this magic in which we have been imprisoned.

JOAQUIN SABINA

Don't give up, please, don't give in, even if the cold burns, even if fear bites, even if the sun hides and the wind shuts up.

MARIO BENEDETTI

Be careful when casting out your demons, don't go throw away the best of yourself.

FRIEDRICH NIETZSCHE

Things I Cannot Say

The crash of two planes against the towers of the World Trade Center opened the gates of hell.

A brutal massacre, the result of a surprise terrorist attack on American soil, was inconceivable. *That would never happen.* However, on September 11, 2001, hatred turned into a beast, rose through the air, and attacked New York—angrily demolishing its symbolic towers, turning them into a couple of bonfires. All the efforts of the firefighters, security agents, and rows of men to vanquish the resulting fire were in vain. With their lungs full of smoke, wounded hands in pain and fingers falling off, they were doomed to defeat. In the end, hatred won. It took only seventy-three minutes to bring down the first skyscraper and twenty-nine more for the second one to hit the ground. The initial impact of the collision was enough to weaken the steel bars that supported the floors and tear apart the columns of a structure that rose one hundred and ten stories each—allegedly designed to withstand fires and natural disasters. Signs of the beast's triumph were the mangle of scorched bodies, of human pieces washed away among thousands of tons of rubble, building materials, mud, glass, fiber, lead, mercury, and the release of dioxins and hydrocarbons in the fires that burned for the following three months.

No one expected to experience or witness a disaster that ended the lives of thousands of people: 2,996 dead (including the 19 terrorists, and the passengers traveling on the E-line subway train, whose bodies were found floating in the water that filled the tunnels under the World Trade Center buildings) and 6,000 injured were reported by agents of the *New York Joint Terrorism Task Force* investigative team.

"Guys, go back to your seats; quit fooling around!" Elina Cano ordered her students. It was 9:05 a.m. on September 11.

"Teacher, that must be a big fire because the smoke is thick and black," insisted one of the students, alarmed and still at the window.

"Calm down; the firefighters will do their job," she said, trying to ease their minds, but then she herself was shocked to see the black cloud invading the sky in the distance.

Unable to explain what was happening, she felt a void in her stomach— the same one she felt whenever something bad was about to happen. Her hands trembled as she wrote on the blackboard and, as best she could, tried to hide the fear squeezing her intestines.

It was 9:35 a.m. when the voice of the principal of the George Washington Educational Campus announced through the speakers that classes were suspended due to an accident in Lower Manhattan. Without explanation, the principal asked the teachers to accompany their students to the auditorium until their parents arrived to pick them up. At 10:00 a.m., Elina Cano and Frank Green, another teacher, went to the cafeteria located in the building next to the school. When they entered the establishment, they found the patrons looking dumbfounded at the images on the giant television screen where the events at hand were being reported live. They learned that, at 8:46 a.m., a plane had crashed into the North Tower of the World Trade Center's Financial Center. The news anchor reported that the impact of American Airlines Boeing 767 Flight 11 had opened a gap between the 93rd and 99th floors, killing hundreds and leaving hundreds more trapped in the flames caused by the burning fuel. Until then, it was believed that the crash had been an accident. But, when at 9:03 a.m., a second plane, another Boeing 767 (United Airlines Flight 175), crashed between the 77th and 85th floors of the South Tower, it became clear that the United States was the victim of an attack.

From that moment, the TV screens of North America filled with images both intense and macabre. Firefighters (prevented by the disruption of elevator service) had difficulty moving forward. Yet, determined to save the lives of those trapped, they climbed the impossibly high stairs. From the burning balconies above, one could see bodies falling—men, women, couples joined in loving yet fatal embrace …. who chose the void over being charred alive.

On the morning of September 11, George W. Bush, the forty-third U.S. president, was visiting the second-grade class of a school in Sarasota, Florida when he was informed of the terrible news. Minutes later, Andrew Card, Chief of staff of the Department of Defense, whispered in his right ear: "A second plane hit the towers. America is under attack." At 9:30 a.m.,

President Bush announced that the country had suffered "a terrorist attack."

There was no doubt anymore: someone was trying to hurt and destroy the empire that controlled half the world. It had to be acknowledged that the enemy, still faceless, had attacked suddenly, with the element of surprise, and the intention was to mercilessly punish the American people.

At 9:37 a.m., a third plane, a Boeing 757, American Airlines Flight 77, crashed into the Pentagon. The Pentagon was a massive concrete and steel building located in Virginia, headquarters to the United States Department of Defense. It would later be known that the flight covered the Washington–Los Angeles route with fifty-eight passengers and six crew members. Without appeasing its fury, the beast attempted to attack once again: at 10:03 a.m., United Airlines Flight 93 from Newark to San Francisco, with thirty-eight passengers and seven crew members, crashed near Shanksville, Pennsylvania, after some passengers (aware of the previous attacks through their cell phones) heroically engaged and subdued the hijackers—forcing the plane down off target. Trying to curb further disasters, the Federal Aviation Administration opted to cancel air operations at all airports in the country, the White House was evacuated, and the stock exchange was ordered closed.

Elina Cano was, in appearance at least, an even-handed person. She resorted to logic as a necessary means and, to avoid getting hurt, often put on a mask of indifference and disdain. Provocative, she repeated that emotions were a deficiency of the brain that exposed our weaknesses. She added that "compassion hides contempt for the useless. Tolerance is a disgusting act to save face, and hope is but a symbol of defeat and resignation."

According to her brother, Elina was incapable of getting upset about the things that took place around her, make important decisions, or commit to anything—so he nicknamed her "Oblomov," comparing her to the shallow character by Russian writer Ivan Goncharov. However, to Frank Green's surprise, at 9:59 a.m., when the South Tower collapsed, Elina, unable to hide her feelings, herself collapsed on the dining table, her eyes filled with tears.

New York, the Capital of the World, the Steel Babel, the Big Apple, the modern, thriving, cosmopolitan city, sank before the bewildered and terrified gaze of its people. At ten o'clock in the morning came the order: the evacuation of all members of the Fire Department from the North Tower. Although many hurried to exit the trampled buildings, some did not heed the call, while others remained unaware of the danger. Twenty-nine minutes later, 10:28 a.m., the North Tower collapsed too. Lower Manhattan and Chinatown were swallowed by the thick cloud mix of smoke, dust and toxic waste that would later be known as "World Trade Center Disease." It was the cause of future respiratory, digestive, and cardiovascular problems, as well as mental disorders, that would years later lead to the death of hundreds of men who participated in the rescue operations.

At 8:20 in the morning N.V. Malo called the offices of *Windows on the World* to apologize for not being able to attend that day to fulfill his duties, with the excuse of feeling sick. N.V. Malo served as a waiter for the food complex's meetings and entertainment events located on the 106th and 107th floors of the North Tower of the World Trade Center. After spending the night drinking with relatives from his native Cuba, N.V. Malo barely managed to wake up. He got out of bed at two o'clock in the afternoon and that's when he learned of the attacks on the Twin Towers. He thought he was inside a nightmare when he saw on the television screen the buildings engulfed in flames and then their collapse. He cried and screamed, horrified by the images, and the pain of knowing he was alive when all his companions had probably perished in the tragedy. That morning he was supposed to be part of the team in charge of serving snacks and lunch to Christine Olender, assistant manager of the restaurant, and to ninety-one attendees of a conference organized by the financial information firm Risk Waters.

N.V. Malo panicked and felt guilty when he heard on the news the information offered by Officer Ray Murray: "From nine o'clock in the morning, for twelve minutes, Mrs. Christine Olender was calling the police department asking for help. The smoke was getting thicker, and she needed to know where to take her guests. Because of the fire caused by the crash of an airplane on the lower floors of the North Tower, the doors were locked, and the elevators stopped working. Christine Olender and the entourage were trapped."

On her last call, in a trembling voice, she said: "This is Christine again, from Windows on the World on the 106th floor. The situation is rapidly worsening. We, we have . . . the air is running out! I'm not exaggerating."

"Um, ma'am, I know you're not exaggerating. We're getting a lot of these calls. Quiet, quiet, we will send the firefighters upstairs as soon as possible."

Distraught, Mrs. Olender had asked:

"What can we do to get the air in? Can we break a window?"

"Whatever you have to do to, uh . . . to get fresh air."

"Okay," Christine said.

Christine Olender and her guests were never heard from again.

A.G. Vallejo was a young man recently arrived from Peru. He was of a melancholy nature and aspired to become a writer. His head was full of ideas, characters, and stories that would soon be captured on paper. He never imagined that he would live in his own flesh an episode worthy of a horror tale.

That Tuesday morning, like any other day at the end of the summer, without any merit to highlight it, he got off the E train at 7:50. He had ten minutes to buy coffee at the World Trade Center, get to 99 John Street and go up to the 25th floor, where he and his colleagues organized the work for the day. At 8:50 a.m., workers heard the voice of Howard Stern, the famous self-proclaimed "King of All Media" on the radio: *I don't want to interrupt the fun, but this is serious news. A plane has exploded into the World Trade Center.* Alarmed, Vallejo exclaimed, "It can't be!"

In the company of Rodolfo Chavez, he went down to the lobby, where he found more people shocked by the images on the television screens. Incredulous, Vallejo went out to the street and looked up at the towers—right at the moment when the second plane kamikazed into the second building. He thought it was a repetition of what he'd seen on TV.

People, amid screams, cries, prayers, and accusations, started to run. "Let's see what's going on," he stupidly said to Chavez and, together, they walked to the corner of John and Cliff streets to buy a camera with the idea of collecting evidence. Vallejo and Chavez advanced to Zuccotti Park, about eighty meters from the towers, where they captured terrifying images. "We began to see bodies falling into the void. Halfway down, we realized they were spinning and losing their clothes, then appeared to accelerate like projectiles until they bounced off the concrete, completely amorphous by then," Vallejo declared later. Suddenly, a dry, mechanical, and synchronized bang was heard. Vallejo turned his gaze to the South Tower, saw the explosion on top of the building (it looked like fireworks) and then felt the ground shake under his feet. "Run, run!" Chavez shouted, but Vallejo did not run. The earth shook, Vallejo fell, and many others fell on him. He managed to stand up, but fell again—driven this time by the shockwave and the collapse of the building.

The falling structure knocked him to the ground and almost buried him alive. Luckily, he was pushed under a truck next to a pile of debris.

It is impossible to fathom the strength despair grants us, but I must be alive thanks to it. For my body was caked, and my skin turned into a crust of sand and lime, Vallejo thought, standing up. Along with other people, holding hands and stumbling upon bodies scattered everywhere, he arrived at Chase Manhattan Plaza. The group entered through the side door of the Federal Reserve Building, where many others had found refuge.

It was chaos. Fear, despair, bewilderment, and panic grew. There were people who didn't know what was going on. There were rumors of a bomb. Vallejo sat on the floor; a boy sat next to him and said, "We're going to die."

"No, it is not true, but we're going to have to live with this forever," Vallejo replied. A few minutes passed, and another rumble was heard all over the place.

It was 10:28 in the morning and the North Tower was collapsing. The impact broke the glass on the windows, blew open the doors, and, again, elicited screams of despair. Vallejo ran outside. On his way out, he found a man who looked like a piece of junk, his face blackened by the smoke and bleeding from his forehead. He was a firefighter.

"Where are you going?" Vallejo asked.

"To the towers," the man answered and then got lost within the thick curtain of smoke from which Vallejo was trying to escape. Along with thousands of people, he crossed the Brooklyn Bridge on foot. Once in lower Brooklyn, people greeted them with bread, bottles of water, and towels to wipe their faces. Vallejo sat down to catch his breath, just for a moment, and then took the train to Jamaica, Queens. On the train, he heard a conversation between two young men.

"They knocked them down, brother," said one, and the other replied, "That's right. And with dynamite."

The clock struck 1:04 p.m. President George W. Bush, at Barksdale Air Force Base, Louisiana, *vowed to pursue and punish those responsible*. The president also said that the military was on high alert around the world.

Osama bin Laden, founder of the Islamic militant organization al-Qaeda, was suspected of being behind the attacks. At 3:25 in the afternoon, building number 7, with forty floors, collapsed—its structure had been weakened by the previous shockwaves.

President George W. Bush was back at the White House when he addressed the nation at 8:30 p.m. The television cameras showed a serene, confident man—self-aware of being in control. Modulating his words, he read a speech designed to cause shock, provoke pain, sadness, anger, desires for revenge . . . and to bring out the patriotism of his fellow citizens. In his dissertation, he said, "Terrorist attacks can shake the foundations of our tallest buildings, but they cannot touch the foundations of America. These attacks can destroy the steel in our buildings, but they cannot break the steel of American determination. America has come under attack because we are the brightest advocate of freedom and opportunity in the world. And no one will be able to make that flame stop shining." Nine days later, on September 20, George W. Bush declared *war on terror*. He did so in a speech of less than seven minutes, with both Houses of the U.S. Congress as spectators. To emphasize his policy, he said: "Whoever is not with us is against us," echoing the words of the Christ, found in Luke 11:23. Adrian Mac Liman, international political analyst, commented that, with this short speech, the president confused the American people and many

Westerners by claiming that the enemy was the Islamists and not the al-Qaeda group. This speech led to new laws being passed and different offices being created, such as the Department of Homeland Security and Immigration and Customs Enforcement.

Osama bin Laden, head of al-Qaeda, slowly drank his whitish mixture of Yeni Raki and water while thinking about the United States. Like many, he cursed the imperialists and had different motives for hating that country. Bin Laden did not forgive the presence of American troops in Saudi Arabia, the support it provided to Israel, or the sanctions against the people of Iraq. The United States displayed despotic, arrogant behavior, but, he said to himself, it is a *paper tiger.* He recalled when, in 1983, the Americans escaped from Lebanon after the bombing of the barracks in Beirut, where 241 Marines on duty died; the withdrawal from Somalia in 1993 (after the death of 18 soldiers in Mogadishu); and the dishonorable withdrawal from Vietnam in the seventies.

In 1996, Osama bin Laden met Khalid Sheikh Mohammed in Tora Bora, Afghanistan. Khalid Sheikh Mohammed, a native of Pakistan, was then a young man of thirty-two years, with dark eyes and a thick black beard. At the age of sixteen, he became an active member of the Muslim Brotherhood, went to study in the United States, where, in 1986, he graduated in Mechanical Engineering from North Carolina Agricultural & Technical State University. After living for years with his fellow Americans, getting to know the American culture and way of life, the young man concluded that the United States was a perverse and racist country. Khalid traveled to Pakistan and later to Afghanistan, where he joined the forces fighting in the jihad/holy war to defeat the invasion of the Soviet Union—seen as an act of aggression against Islam. Khalid admired Osama bin Laden's oratory skills, his ability to manipulate a variety of strategies and easily get his message across—even to the ignorant. According to the Commission appointed by President G.W. Bush and the U.S. Congress to investigate the 9/11 attacks, it was during the meeting in Afghanistan that Khalid Sheikh Mohammed presented Osama bin Laden with the plan for an operation involving the training of pilots to crash planes into buildings in the United States. The Commission of Inquiry reported that al-Qaeda provided the money, personnel, and logistics support to execute the plan. It was bin Laden who decided to put the project in the hands of Mohammed Atta, an experienced kidnapper, and his group of Western-educated jihadists. The hijackers, the majority from Saudi Arabia, traveled in small groups to settle in the United States and receive pilot training on commercial flights.

On September 17, six days after the abominable attacks, President G.W. Bush announced that he wanted Osama bin Laden captured "Dead or Alive." A reward of twenty-five million dollars was offered for information about the whereabouts of the terrorist leader. Many years later, after a long chase by U.S. security agencies through the territories of Afghanistan and Pakistan, bin Laden was found in a garrison in the Pakistani city of Abbottabad. During the early hours of May 2, 2011, under the orders of President Barack Obama, a small group Navy SEALS stormed his lair. They shot and killed Osama bin Laden, *the mastermind* behind the Terrorist Attacks of September 11.

The attacks left deep wounds. The pain, anxiety, terror could not be compared to anything experienced in the past. The American people stopped feeling they were in the safest nation in the world. Knowing that the enemy could enter the country, blow up buildings, and murder thousands of people caused panic and generated xenophobia against the Muslim population. To restore confidence and tranquility to the citizens and, more than anything, to secure its geostrategic position, the government initiated a direct war with Iraq, started new conflicts in the Middle East, bombed Afghanistan, and developed new rhetoric about the forces of good against evil. During the months of 2002, the Federal Bureau of Investigation (FBI), the Central Intelligence Agency (CIA), the National Commission on Terrorist Attacks Upon the United States (9/11 Commission), and the National Institute of Standards and Technology of the United States Department of Commerce (NIST) conducted a series of investigations to determine the circumstances surrounding the attacks, in an attempt to show that there was nothing to fear, that nothing could bring down the empire, that, against all odds, the United States continued to control the world.

Based on the inconsistencies between the investigations and the government version of the events, suspicious people expressed their distrust: "Something's not right. They are deceiving us; they're hiding something from us. It is not possible that the crash of an airplane and a fire could bring down buildings as strong as the Twin Towers. They were not card castles. It makes no sense that an airplane could approach the Pentagon without activating the anti-aircraft defenses . . . ." Theories began to circulate that members of the government were already aware of al-Qaeda's plans but had done nothing to prevent them. Other theories accused the government itself of planning and carrying out the attacks.

In the book *Unmasking September 11*, David Ray Griffin, American Professor of Philosophy of Religion and Theology (Claremont University of California), and author of several books of social and political content, made a point-by-point analysis of the facts and claimed to find at least 51 serious flaws in the official version. According to this publication, there was no independent investigation of the facts. What became public domain was the report of a political commission chaired by Philip Zelikow, an employee of the Bush administration.

At first, David Ray Griffin was reluctant to believe in the political games of an elite group and the possible complicity of the government in terrorist attacks to start wars in favor of their political-economic interests. He pondered, "Was it a coincidence that just before the 9/11 attacks, Cathleen P. Black, who had connections to the CIA and the Pentagon, president of the Hearst magazine emporium (*Cosmopolitan, Esquire, Harper's Bazaar*, etc.) and owner of *Popular Mechanics*, fired her chief editor and other crucial staff members, and hired, in their stead, James Meigs and Benjamin Chertoff—nephew of Michael Chertoff, strongman of the Bush administration?"

This is what Griffin wondered upon discovery that Meigs and Chertoff were responsible for producing the official 9/11 report. Then, he set out to disrupt what, for him, was a farce, and bring the truth to light.

Griffin claimed that the two towers did not collapse. They imploded and disintegrated—as was the case with Building 7, which was not rammed by any aircraft.

In January 2004, Larry Silverstein, owner of Building 7 and tenant of the World Trade Center, during the *America Rebuilds* television interview on PBS, commented that, in a call from the fire department commander, to inform that he was not sure they could contain the fire in Building 7, he had said to the commander, "We have already had a terrible loss of life; perhaps the smartest thing to do is to pull it."

At 3:25 p.m., Tower 7 fell, pulverized. Griffin explained that a sudden, total disintegration of solid buildings and constructions could only occur via controlled demolition processes.

Griffin argued that the damage caused by the planes and the limited fires that followed could not explain the disintegration of the buildings. The huge steel skeletons of the towers possessed a gigantic device that absorbed and eliminated heat produced by limited fires. According to NIST's final report, the steel available for examination reached temperatures above 250 degrees Celsius (482 degrees Fahrenheit). It should be noted, Griffin said, that a home oven reaches higher temperatures than that and the oven neither melts nor deforms. Steel begins to melt at 1500 degrees Celsius (2732 degrees Fahrenheit), indicating that the explanation for the collapse of the towers because of the heat-weakened steel was false. After interviewing firefighters, police, surviving tenants and witnesses to the tragedy, Griffin provided their statements claiming to have heard a series of explosions prior to the disintegration of the buildings. Those testimonies were ignored and silenced by investigators of the official report.

The evidence offered by the government about the Boeing 757 of American Airlines Flight 77 that hit the

Pentagon were the remains of the bodies they said they'd found. However, nothing else was reported. They found no suitcases, the black box, traces of the fuselage, the wings, the seats . . . nothing. The plane was a hundred-thousand-pound machine, but, to this day, it remains unexplained whatever happened with the huge mass of molten aluminum and large pieces of steel and titanium that made up the engines and should have been sitting somewhere. The official report recorded that this was due to *the vaporization of the metal due to the speed of impact and intense fire.* Logically, Griffin wondered, "How then do you explain the recovery of bodies with flesh and blood?"

Thierry Meyssan, a French journalist, director of the Voltaire Network website, in his book *The Great Imposture,* questioned the official version in three sections:

I. *A bloody staging:* The attacks were an internal plot aimed at changing opinions and forcing the course of events.

II.   *Death to Democracy in the United States*: The war in Afghanistan was not a response to the attacks but a long-coming plan in collaboration with the British. *The War on Terror* was a ruse to suspend individual freedoms in the United States and allied countries.

III.   *The empire attacks*: Osama bin Laden was a CIA fabrication. The bin Laden and Bush families managed their estate together through the Carlyle Group. At the right time, they sacrificed bin Laden as they would a lab rat. The CIA developed a program of intervention at all levels that included the use of torture and political assassination.

Meyssan's theory coincided with that of the American Griffin regarding the strange, perfectly vertical collapse of the Twin Towers and that of building 7. This type of collapse had never occurred in the case of large constructions due to the sole effect of fire, which suggested the work of engineers specializing in the destruction of buildings using explosives. *The Open Chemical Physics Journal* published the results of research conducted by nine scientists led by Niels H. Harrit, a professor in the department of chemistry at the University of Copenhagen, Denmark. After a year and a half of investigation in the laboratory, particles of an explosive called *nano thermite* were found in different dust samples collected at four different points in Manhattan—just after the attacks. Some of the explosive particles were one millimeter in diameter, therefore observable with the naked eye.

Meyssan went so far as to compare 9/11 to the burning of the Reichstag by the Nazis, which allowed Hitler to blame the Bulgarian communists and impose a dictatorship under the pretext of defending democracy against terrorism.

Since its inauguration on September 11, 2011, a pair of reflector pools surrounded by bronze panels with the names of the attack victims occupies the place where the Towers stood. At the underground level, a museum was built where objects found in the rubble are exhibited—as well as personal effects that the victims used in everyday life. *One World Trade Center* is the name of the building inaugurated on November 3, 2014 to replace the Towers. This monument was built not to lament the facts but to prevent the horror, outrage, and nightmare experienced that September day from being forgotten. According to Cano, Green, Vallejo, and many other followers of the theories of Griffin and Meyssan, history will record the facts according to the official version, which the powers-that-were decided was convenient and adjusted to bureaucratic interests. The other version will be recorded as fiction—theories by a few overzealous conspirators. The world will never really know which version was real or fraudulent. History will follow its dirty and absurd cycles, as always, indifferent to pain, manipulations, deceptions, and the deaths of thousands of innocent people. As President

Barack Obama said five years after bin Laden's assassination: "The world is still dangerous." There is no doubt that this will be the case, think the followers of the theorists; the world will remain insecure and afraid because the elimination of an individual does not suppress the hatred, ambition and greed sown in the hearts of the people. Perhaps good intentions can combat negative feelings, and what Obama said serves as a guideline, "We have chosen hope over fear, unity of purpose over conflict and discord."

"Son, that's how I do it. The thing is, when I do it, everything turns out perfect." That's what Mom always says, and these same words come to mind as I listen to my sister's anguished voice over the phone, complaining to me about our mother's insufferable attitude.

Mom is a pain in the ass. She wants to do things her own damn way. She can't accept that I, my sister, and other people can do things, too—possibly even better than her. Quite often, I let her get away with it only to avoid conflict—even if later I have to redo what she's done. I'm not sure whether things are as bad with Mom as Gilly says they are, or this is another one of Mom's strategies to make herself important.

For years, Mom has suffered from vertigo. Whenever she had a crisis, she'd say, "Son, this is it, this is the end." At first, I would get scared. I was distraught at the idea of losing her. However, after so many *definitive* episodes (in which nothing serious ever happened), I started to make fun of her: "This is the season finale, this is the end of the chapter, the conclusion of the story." Our mom—Elina—is a difficult, contradictory woman who's failed to understand herself. She enjoys being the villain of the film, the black sheep of the flock, the witch of the story . . . . She loves to attract attention, enjoys knowing that people talk about her even if only to criticize and tear her to pieces. I have come to think that, in addition to being an egomaniac with histrionic capabilities, and a mythomaniac, she is also a masochist. She enjoys being skinned alive. She likes people to say mean things about her. Sure, again, she's made one of her silly acts and then resorted to those idiotic theories that she herself does not believe, but says are part of the path she is destined to travel. "Why did you say that? Why did you do such a thing? Did you do it on purpose?" I have scolded her a few times, when she's come groaning like a cornered dog, begging me to help her get out of the mess she has gotten into for not knowing how to control herself.

"Son, I could not help it. What should have happened, happened," she'll say; and that's her escape route from guilt, responsibilities, and, above all else, to protect her ego. Usually, people defend themselves in any way they can, arguing through truths or lies—whatever gets them out of a mess. Not Mom, no. She must rationalize everything and, just like Aesop's fox, makes up a reassuring explanation to hide her frustration at not reaching the grapes.

"The grapes were green!" Mom says and dismisses it all according to her convenience. She disdains the virtue implied in man's willpower—that characteristic which allows us to be in control of our actions and decisions. She calls "resigned animals" (without faith in themselves) those who leave everything to God: *It's in God's hands*. Aristotle argued that if we accept certain assumptions about the nature of truth, then the future is already determined. Likewise, Nietzsche proposed *amor fati*, the love of destiny, the philosophy of predeterminism—in which people are necessarily predestined to repeat the same events an infinite number of times over an infinite period of time. For her own benefit and defense, Mom relies on these fatalistic philosophical doctrines: "Nothing happens fortuitously. Whatever is meant to happen is waiting for us; everything is fixed and takes place out of necessity."

I have refuted her often and defended my views: that we are not and cannot be mastered by any supreme force outside of our own will. I tell her, "Accept your mistakes and weaknesses; stop looking for explanations in defeatist reasoning that does not go with you. Your submissive attitude is a violation of free will." Wasted time! Mom is the triumph of rationalism and contradiction. It is due to such nonsense that Gilly's voice sounds so anguished.

"Adrian, Mom is in the hospital. She's under observation as we speak. Doctors are running tests and analyses. This morning, Jack and I went to her apartment and found her comatose. She couldn't speak or move and could barely open her eyes You know what Mom is like. She'd do anything to screw with us, but this time I fear she is really sick." My sister spoke with a grunt and a gasp, as if it were hard for her to speak. I was stuck in devilish traffic along Queens Boulevard. The day so far had been a complicated one, and now this. As I tried to maneuver my way out of the jam, I pictured Gilly trembling, looking for an open door, a hole through which she could run away. She must have been holding back, so as not to scream until she got deeply disgruntled, and—like a cat someone has seized against its will—she'd started to kick and scratch to get rid of the pain.

Gilly is a sensible woman. She tests the ground before moving forward, plans things, and acts in such a way that the results are generally favorable. More than anything, Gilly is intuitive. Oftentimes, I have come to suspect that she is a witch—if it is true that we have past lives, my sister must have been a prophet or a pythoness. However, she does not know how to face and handle hard, stressful situations. People who do not know her tend to misjudge her. They believe Gilly to be rude and aggressive—but her insults, hurtful words, and despicable attitude are but a shield. It's how she protects herself from getting hurt.

Gilly is six years older than me, but, somehow, even though she calls me *my baby brother*, it seems like it's the other way around. Therefore, I am obliged to protect and pamper her. There were many unsettling things and bitter moments we had to live through and overcome together. That's why I am patient, understanding—I endure her mood swings, rants, and tantrums. If it were not so, I would have already sent her to go fuck herself more than once.

I remember being seven when Gilly scraped her knees and hands on the pavement while attempting to run with roller skates on. Mom poured iodine on the wounds, covered them with band aids, and then blamed it on me. "Look at your poor sister, crying because of you. You had to watch out for her and help her. You were born to take care of her!" I hated her at that moment. I felt a terrible desire to grab her by the neck and strangle her. I was a child, but she was already placing this responsibility on me that by all means was hers. She was the one to take care of my sister and me. She was the adult, the mother. But no, fuck that! She wouldn't!

When I turned nine, Mom enrolled me in catechism classes—according to her, so that I would learn about the vile falsehoods of Christianity and not let myself be surprised when they came to me with infamous, immoral, and stupid stories about a god who was also a dove, and a megalomaniac Christ who raised the dead and loved himself more than anything in the world: "I am the good shepherd, I am the bread of life, I am the light of this world, I am the resurrection and eternal life, I . . . I . . . I . . ."

In those classes, I heard the biblical tale of Cain and Abel, the two miserable and wretched brothers. With them, I discovered injustice, arbitrariness, and tyranny (I was angry at Mom again for acting just like that despotic, wicked, and ridiculous god.) Am I my sister's keeper? No, I'm not. But I try to protect her because I simply love Gilly and feel, just like her, the emptiness left by the lack of attention and care from our selfish and irresponsible mother. I think my atheism was born in that moment of anger and disappointment, in finding fault with beings supposed to have no flaws. I stopped believing in the existence of a perfect being when I found not only inconsistencies, but lack of evidence in the doctrines imposed by the church. David Hume was right when he said: *Everything pertinent to human knowledge, in this deep and dark ignorance, needs to be treated with skepticism or, at least, caution; and not to admit any hypothesis, anyone; much less, everything supported by any semblance of probability.* It is humiliating for me to meet people who blindly respond to the teachings of the *holy men chosen by God* and the alleged truths revealed in the scriptures without stopping to think and use reasoning and logic. Cowardly fools! They leave everything in the hands of strangers (human and imagined) rather than face reality. I can't say what Mom's position was on this matter because she repudiated and shouted against everything and everyone.

I have never been able to pigeonhole or define that woman life gave me for a mother. Against all odds, she claimed to be a free thinker, an atheist. However, she accepted that her two children be baptized in compliance with the rites imposed by Catholicism. And Mom also agreed with certain Jewish traditions. It was the only way to understand why she would allow the damn practice of *brit milah* for which I lost my foreskin days after I was born. Mom met with experts in agnosticism, attended the magical rituals of sorcery, practiced tarot reading, and for a short time dabbled in the interpretation of the Kabbalah. It was as if she were looking for something to believe in or at least something to identify with without recognizing that her nihilism ruled over her and did not allow her to cling to a safe board in the wide-open ocean where one day she would sink. Outside of herself, there was nothing worthwhile.

"That's how I do it" was the phrase she used to indicate that only what she did was the right thing to do and that she was unwilling to consider or approve of anything different from her opinion. Whatever project or job I presented to her, her answer was the same, "*Mijo,* it is not that I think it's wrong or don't like it, but you could do the same thing another way." By that she meant her way, always her way. That is why religion, dogmas, society, God, and love failed her. That's why everything failed her.

She allowed Jehovah's witnesses to enter the house when they knocked on our door. She did not do it with the intention of talking, of knowing their reasoning; she was not even interested in dissuading them, much less debating them because, well, she already knew her position, her reality, beforehand—and that was the only valid thing. If she invited them to come in, it was to screw with them. With a condescending and good-natured smile that could confuse anyone, Mom pretended to listen, as the poor individuals took on the task of preaching *the truth* and the love of the Maker of the World. Mom allowed them to elaborate until, suddenly, in a hurry, she'd shoot them a question, "Do you know or can you give me any evidence of his existence?" Believers never hesitate to answer that the mere observation of nature is sufficient manifestation of his divine presence. Trained to counter and not give up, one of them used that famous argument of "the Designer" to explain that the world (particularly, the living organisms on Earth) was too complex to be the result of a natural mechanism or to have come out of nowhere. "Let's suppose," said the unwary one, "that we are going down a secluded road and find a clock. Its complicated mechanism indicates that it is an artifact designed with a purpose; likewise, the universe and existence are evidence of the complex design made by a supreme being."

Mom, with studied calm, answered, "I look around and realize that every living system, or not, follows a natural process of organization. In fact, nothing is necessary outside of simple and basic physical and chemical processes. If one of God's qualities was to design the universe for the purpose of making life, especially human life, then the flaws we observe in this design lead us to think that a god with this condition cannot exist. I must explain that the parts of a human body are nothing like those of a watch, which are exquisitely designed by an expert. This human mechanism would need the intervention of an engineer to fix it and make it work for an extended period of time if expected to function with any degree of reasonable results. If we can enjoy a long life compared to that of other species, it is thanks to the fact that our evolution resulted in offspring that need years to mature. I think it doesn't make sense to continue talking about a design in this world where there is so much miserable imperfection." I admit that I enjoyed watching Mom make the sheep sweat.

"Now I ask you another question: If this god is so powerful, why did he need six days to create the world when he could have done it in less than a thousandth of a second? You don't have to answer because now I'm about to tell you something that will make you think and reason. You probably know that the universe has existed for more than thirteen billion years, the Earth for four and a half billion, and humans, as we know them today, for two hundred thousand years. Why did your god waste so much time and, instead of the six days the Bible claims, waited more than nine billion years to make the Earth and then another four billion to finally create man?"

Generally, Mom spoke pure crap. However, she could make surprising comments and cite great quotes and interesting facts thanks to the reading and rereading of authors such as Brian Greene, Paul Davies, or Victor Stenger. She adored Neil deGrasse Tyson, the scientific director of the New York City Planetarium, who advertises himself as *your personal astrophysicist*. For her, everything Tyson says is written in stone. After the poor Jehovah's Witnesses had fled in horror, she commented, "Delusional! They have nothing else to do in life except walk from house to house convinced that God enlightens them and thinking they will convince others with their fantasies. It satisfies me to expose them a little, to corner them . . . to leave them butt naked, their asses in the air."

Mom was definitely full of crap. She could simultaneously defend and condemn a particular position. She stood for anything—went with the flow. One of her friends was Tony Arcos, another troublemaker like her, a guitarist, and the last communist on the face of the Earth. Gilly and I nicknamed him *Wolverine* because he had nails like claws he let grow so that he could tear the strings off the guitar. By his side, she joined every street march, carrying posters and chanting proclamations—not because she believed in the causes, but because she enjoyed the uproar. She formed lines supporting the rights of undocumented immigrants while, on the other hand, she declared that the government should strengthen security at the borders so that no more undesirable people entered the country. Carrying one of the banners reading: "We are the 99%," she joined the groups stationed at Zuccotti Park in the financial district to denounce economic inequality in the United States, and yet celebrated people's ability and cunning to accumulate fortunes. She participated in the "Flood Wall Street" demonstrations that took place near the famous "charging bull" against the role of capitalism in climate change. All the while, she claimed that global warming was a natural process of the planet.

"Jack and I found her lying on her bed with her eyes closed and an expression of strange serenity on her face." Gilly's voice takes me out of my thoughts and returns me to reality. "She looked as if she were fast asleep. She could hear us though. As if it were hard for her, she opened her eyes. She could not or did not want to speak to us." I don't respond because a feeling of suffocation squeezes my chest as I think of the woman who brought me into the world. On top of that, the driver behind me blares his horn and seems about to crash into my trunk. I lift my head out the window to mouth a *Fuck you* at him.

"We arrived at her apartment to take her out of the cave for a while. You know what our mother is like. Most of the time, she refuses to share time with us because she simply does not feel like it and uses her precious books as pretext—the ones she reads and the ones she writes. I confess that, many times, I felt like setting them on fire. Then, maybe, she would finally notice me. It's because of the damn books she is going blind—she's using a magnifying glass on top of her prescription lenses." Gilly complains through sobs she's unable to control. "Fortunately, I'd convinced Jack to come with me. He was in charge of calling 911," Gilly said.

Mom was not sick per se. She suffered from the ailments pertinent to her age—nothing to worry about. From time to time, she would get vertigo attacks or walk with a limp due to the recurrent pain in her hips. "Doctors are trying to determine the cause of her condition; it is possible that she had a minor stroke. Her current state of health could be the product of lack of food or even an overdose of medication. Lately, she hasn't been eating well enough. She also complained about not remembering having taken her medicines, and it was possible she ingested more pills than prescribed," says Gilly. At that moment, listening to her complaints, I think I made a mistake by not even entertaining my brother-in-law's suggestions. Jack had recommended that we seek the help of a woman who could take care of *the mama*. "A Mexican or a Guatemalan, one of those women who abound in these places and who work happily for a few dollars would be the ideal person to accompany her," Jack said, reminding me of the burden that weighed me down: Mom was my responsibility, too.

It was not like Mom was in the last stages of her life, nah. She could fend for herself for a few more years. The problem was that she lived alone and was a fool. "Mom, you need someone to keep you company, to help you," we had told her.

"Do you think I'm useless? In need of a nanny who wipes my mouth and cleans my ass?" she replied and added that she resented the house arrest, the loneliness to which my sister had condemned her when she convinced her to move to that cemetery called Florida where the Jewish mummies went to leave their bones. Then she remembered that her own mother, the Toby, always repeated to her and her siblings that they had been born alone, that alone they had to face life, and alone they would one day die.

"You're full of crap. All you do is pure theatrics—and lousy theatrics at that," I said. "What loneliness are you talking about? You love to wander, be surrounded by people. If you had your druthers, you would live on the street, in a park or a bar full of rioters. If you don't leave this cave now, it's out of foolishness."

Mom insisted on showing Gilly that in Florida there was no life, that in Florida there was no excitement like there was in New York. Mom missed her friends and comrades with whom she shared half a life, those who, according to her, did understand her and made life an exciting adventure. At every chance Mom got, she threw in Gilly's face that, because of her, she endured living in the hell of palm trees and artificial lagoons that was Florida; in that swamp disguised as an impeccable condominium, surrounded by people known only in passing, ridiculous tourists taking photos of ridiculous palm trees, and, above all, the *snowbirds,* those sluggish and puny old people who arrived from New York or Michigan fleeing the cold and snow in the north.

Jack is a big man. His corpulence is intimidating. Even more so, the tone of his voice; it sounds like the man is using a loudspeaker every time he talks. After meeting him, nevertheless, one realizes that he is not to be feared—his physical appearance and roughness are pure *façade.* Jack is a man of good feelings, a person who can be trusted. Of course, he is not perfect. One must be an idiot to believe that there is a man without blemish—every human being has their dark side, and Jack has his own crap. In addition to being insufferable, Jack is spiteful. He couldn't stand his mother-in-law. And, no wonder, when Mom met him, she made a face at him and told him he was too big and not the man she would have wanted for her daughter.

After he and my sister got married, Jack, a detective in the NYPD, accustomed to intimidating people with his big body and loud voice, declared war on *the mama,* and Mom accepted the challenge, confident in her cunning. "This Sicilian Goliath thinks he can tangle with me," she said, alluding to the size of her son-in-law compared to her own height. Mom is tiny, but her five feet do not prevent her from facing whoever comes looking for trouble. "He may think himself Vito Corleone, but I know my tricks. He may scream with his trumpet voice, but I know how to find the weak side in people and, right there, ha, I'll make him dance the Italian mambo."

Mom called me often. Not to ask about my health or how the family was doing, but to complain about the son-in-law. I tried to calm her down, make her see that, being the most experienced, she should take a step back for Gilly's peace of mind—and everyone else's. A futile effort, as there were no words to coax her into peace-making. "I'm too old to let this Rambo-attitude Sicilian think I am stupid. I'm not allowing that. I will not hold back, and he will know what I am capable of."

To all this, Jack responded by preventing Gilly from seeing Mother, and insisted on getting a woman to care for her or sending her to a nursing home. Anything to get rid of the mother-in-law. If this last plan had not been carried out, it was because Gilly disagreed, "One hears, reads, and sees so many horrible things in newspapers and on television about these places that it is scary to have a loved one in the hands of potentially heartless people. These asylums are real concentration camps where the elderly starve and stink of piss and shit." Thinking about all this tragedy, I tell myself that if Mom emerges victorious from this moment she is going through, she must come back to New York, the city where she spent three quarters of her life and where she actually likes to live.

Mom has her years on her, but she is alert. She keeps her five senses—or, in her case, six or seven senses—in great shape. She has the right to live as she wants, where she wants, and with the people she wants to live with. Mom has said (speaking of New York) that she would never stop marveling, even though she has seen them a thousand times, at the paintings of van Gogh, de Chirico, Dalí, Degas . . . works she found in the Metropolitan Museum. She would forever be enchanted by the fragrance of freedom that, according to her, can only be breathed in the Village, in Central Park. She would never tire of admiring the beauty of the Brooklyn Bridge or the silhouette of New York as seen in the twilight. Mom will not stop enjoying the things she likes just because she is old; that would be like stopping breathing because she knows that one day she will die. As García Márquez said: *It is not true that people stop chasing dreams because they get older; they get old because they stop chasing their dreams.*

My sister is a mature woman, but she does not get Mom. She needs to stop believing that Mom is finished, that the best thing Mom can do is accept she is no longer a *spring chicken* (as Gilly teases her), forget about whims, and stay put wherever she is.

Gilly believes Mom should give up on her desires of continuing with the *parranda*. I know Gilly thinks she wants to protect her when, in fact, that's an excuse to hide her fear of losing the shadow that gives her courage when she doesn't know what to hold on to, the refuge she seeks when alone or lost. Even if it hurts, good or bad, Gilly must finish cutting the umbilical cord, that invisible bond that imprisons her, where she cowers away from the world.

For me, the process of separation was easier; and, at the same time, more painful because it was Mom who, without prior notice, brought the axe down—since I did not yet have enough strength to get rid of the anchor. Mom went with her party elsewhere, and everyone was happy while I was left to endure life as best I could.

Mom didn't have time for us. She had many plans to fulfill: educate herself, make a career, compete. She—as always, believing she was right—argued that what distinguishes us as humans is intelligence, demonstrating that we use our brains.

"Feelings are foolishness. They devalue us. I have too many important things to do. I will not dedicate my life to walking kids in a stroller and cleaning their mouths and asses all day. If I don't get something better now, when am I going to get it?" She rebelled against and complained to both of her ex-husbands, Gilly's father and mine.

I understand that things are difficult, that life gives us nothing for free, and we must bend our backs and grind if we want to enjoy certain comforts. I understand all this perfectly. I also understand that taking care of children, giving them affection, pampering them, teaching them to see danger, to differentiate right from wrong is not a waste of time. Of course, over time, children will learn it all, but it is not the same as to get trained by their own parents.

I do resent always feeling alone—even if the whole world screams happily all around me. I feel this way because of a mother who proudly boasted about having tits like a teenager's because she never breastfed any child. "That's why they invented bottles and formulas with all the necessary nutrients for growth. Breastfeeding? Leave it for the cows. I am a thinking human being." It is curious the fact that, despite her treating us like small animals collected from an adoption center, Gilly and I loved her.

As time went on, I realized that Mom had her reasons for being the way she was. Yet, as a child, all I knew was that I needed her. For me, it was impossible to see myself living without Mom, not to feel, from time to time, her hand slide and ruffle through my hair; how it managed to make me feel like the luckiest child in the world. Mom was the most important thing in my life. Mom was the center of my universe.

"I must go see Mom," I say, avoiding getting sentimental as I try to leave the crazy traffic I am stuck in to find a parking spot. I need to call my wife too. Let her know what's going on.

It's spring. The temperatures have risen to the point that the trees have started turning green again. After a long and harsh winter, people, fed up with the cold and snow, have abandoned coats, boots, hats, and gloves, and taken to the streets to enjoy the warmth the new season's offering. Climate changes, somewhat drastic, make New Yorkers go from one extreme to the other. Only a few weeks ago, we looked like polar bears and now, with a little heat, it is not long before many of us go out naked. In New York, millions of people come from all over the planet, speak their own language, profess their beliefs, and worry about their own affairs. It would be absurd to pay attention to what others do. In this city, there is no room for complexes or inhibitions. That is why no one is surprised to see a fat woman with her belly hanging out of a tiny blouse, the trans in *leggings* and heels, the exhibitionists with shorts that cover only half their asses, the ultra-orthodox Hasidic Jews sheathed in black *halat*, the Middle Eastern women sweating like a pressure cooker inside that black tunic, which, according to Mom, looks like a plastic garbage bag.

I can't say Mom was racist, but she was definitely toxic. Without any respect, she made poisonous comments about everyone: "I imagine the ass-like stench those people of the Middle East must bring glued to their bodies; the Hindus reek of curry, the Blacks of *Cajun fried chicken*, the Chinese of soy sauce, the French of rancid cheese, the Spaniards of chorizo . . . ." To give her a taste of the same poison she spews, I asked her, "Mom, and we

Hispanics smell like baked sofrito and piglet?"

Many are of the opinion that New York is a horrible city. A dirty, bustling, stinking, and dangerous place. Others say New York may be the center of the world, with its museums, theaters, libraries, the Empire State Building, Lincoln or Rockefeller Center . . . and also rats of all kinds all over the place. Your average four-legged rats, in the sewers, fat and huge, running on the tracks of the underground train. And then the two-legged rats (the low human kind) coming from all four sides of the world. The funny thing is that there are many who cast pestilence on the city, but then cry and beg for another chance if the Immigration Department forces them to leave it.

Mom said she was a young woman in her early twenties when she came to this country, to New York, where people were rude and insensitive. Just a couple of weeks later, she got off the subway and found a man lying on the floor, convulsing, and drooling. She was terrified to see how people rushed by to take the train without even noticing the poor man—who seemed to be having an epileptic seizure. At that time, Mom did not speak a shred of English; yet, through signs, gestures, and half-chewed English words, she asked someone to help the poor man. It was a Hispanic woman. She said that was not her *business*. "I don't go around solving other people's problems. I don't have time to waste in court testifying over shit I don't know or getting harassed by the police."

Mom left both the man and the potential lawsuit behind. She panicked the moment she heard the word "police." Over the years, Mom learned to live and let live . . . and die. She learned not to be moved by beggars and filthy people. Since Mom couldn't hold her tongue when facing the human spoils crammed into any street, she said, "Shame on you, lying there like a filthy dog when you were dealt all the winning cards. You were born in this land of opportunity; you speak English. Hell, you are even pretty. If only you knew how hard it is for us, the starving, who came from a miserable country."

Mom got used to seeing, without squealing, the fat, cat-sized rats that strolled on the rails of the subways. She grew immune to the never-ending noise of ambulances, police cars, and the alarm of vehicles that went off either due to carelessness or a bottle thrown by a *scumbag*.

As a now first world woman, Mom adopted the *resting bitch face* that distinguishes New Yorkers and, as a good New Yorker, became direct, insolent, and indifferent to the little things and bullshit that mainly disturb the rest of the world. Waiting for the change of lights, I look at both sides and unwillingly think that "Death Avenue," as we call Queens Boulevard with its twelve lanes (and sixteen in the Forest Hills section), seems rather *the Great Way of the Universe.* People from all over the world parade through it—never caring or concerned about the life of those walking close by.

The traffic lights change to green, and like the other drivers I put my foot on the accelerator and speed on—as if getting to the workplace were a matter of life and death. It's 9:30 in the morning. I'm late. So what? I think. Fuck punctuality! Today I'm going to get nowhere!

Looking at the first flowers poking their heads over the flower beds in the parkways, I think, *this is the worst time to die*. Mom can be ridiculous and extravagant, but not stupid enough to choose a beautiful time like this to end her own life. I don't think Mom overdosed on her pills. That crazy woman likes to attract attention—and, in order to get it, well, she might sell her soul to the devil; but take her own life? Never.

At some point, I suggested that she write her memoirs. It would be interesting to read what Mom has to say about her childhood and adolescence in Ecuador; the anecdotes about her father, my grandfather Juan, "the genius" (who was as crazy as his daughter); the horrendous experiences she was forced to live in this strange and alien country she later made more her own than her native land.

"What a magnificent idea you have given me, Son! Of course, I'm going to write my memoirs. But, since there are things I can't say, I will let others say it. You, Gilly, my sister, and my friends will oversee the progress of my stories. Fantastic! The recounting of my memories will begin with an evil event and the possibility of my death!"

I imagined her dancing, hands on her back, imitating Mick Jagger—jumping with that pair of skinny legs and bunioned feet she has. "You're full of crap!" I blurted out indignantly, as I did every time she came out with her ridiculous genius. "Coward, you are a coward! Always hiding behind others to look good, to avoid responsibilities. What are you afraid of? To talk about your weaknesses, your faults? Be brave and face the truth one damn time." Mom's answer put a plug in my mouth, "Let me do what I want; I am the writer here."

Mom didn't know how to—or couldn't—make suggestions, let alone give recommendations. She never warned us of any danger; however, she allowed Gilly and me to speak openly, to fight mistreatment and thus remove any poison from our souls. That's something I thank her for. She never scolded us like other parents do for saying out loud what we thought—even if the attacks and reproaches were against her. Of course, sometimes she went out of her way because we would overdo our rants, but she still endured the lashes. She wouldn't scold us for being rude either. Instead, she celebrated that we vented. When she heard us swearing left and right, she told us, "Insolence helps empty us of rage and cleanse us inside." Giving us that freedom was her way of telling us that it was okay not to hide what we thought of others—not out of cowardice, but out of respect.

"This is how it should be, not as my parents mistakenly taught me. It's healthy to talk, to say things head-on; it doesn't matter that people dislike us for rubbing their shit under their noses. My siblings and I kept silent even if they were killing us or the world fell on us, just so as not to offend others. That's why they abused us, took advantage of us, and treated us like fools." Mom said those words as she recalled bitter episodes—that now that she has guts, she'd love to live again, just to kick the asses of all the jerks who fucked up her existence.

Mom resented the disgusting way she was treated by the aunt she lived with when she first arrived in New York. "It was as if, instead of being my mother's half-sister, she was an enemy. The old woman believed she had gotten a maid who should obey blindly if she wanted to eat, and, not content with that, she stole the little money I earned working in the so-called 'factories.' Her own children, I, and anyone around her, suffered the consequences of the low self-esteem and resentments that twisted her guts and soul." Knowing how evil this aunt of hers had been to my mom, I was glad to learn I used to call her *The Whore*. Mom told me that, as soon as I started to pronounce my first words, her aunt would repeat, "whore, whore, whore" to me, so that I would insult people—as if swearing were part of a child's grace. *Whore!* I called the aunt when I spoke clearly enough. And when she realized that shit boomeranged its way to her, she would angrily complain to Mom about it. Fortunately, there was no going back because I thought *Whore* was her name—and it was well-deserved.

Mom came to New York during Richard Nixon's administration, which ended with his resignation over the Watergate scandal. During the impeachment process, Nixon was charged with obstruction of justice, criminal cover-up, abuse of power, and complicity in stealing copies of top-secret documents. The *Watergate* affair added still more disappointment to the American people—already embittered by previous hardships and losses, such as the results of the nineteen-year intervention in the Vietnam War and the assassinations of JFK, Robert Kennedy, and Martin Luther King Jr.

During the seventies, immigrants were still welcome. The American nation needed cheap labor for all kinds of merchandise manufactured and assembled in factories. Immigrants, documented or not, did the work that in the nineties the agreements and negotiations of the Free Trade Agreement among the North American countries threw to the ground. NAFTA was the beneficial agreement for owners of industries and companies, and signed by the heads of state—hungry for power. The agreement was intended to remove customs barriers and increase investment opportunities between the three northern countries. Mom said that one should never believe the statements of a politician, for their job is to say tricky words as if these words came from the bottom of their soul. Politicians were akin to the sellers of snake oil that could be found at every other corner in Mom's land. Those tricksters (who claimed to be as gifted as the Nazarene, resurrector of the dead) could convince the most incredulous people about the advantages of their miraculous ointment.

Under the lights of reflectors and cameras, looking straight, without blinking, the charmers of the new nations asked us to read their lips, not their intentions. *Read my lips: no new taxes*, George W. Bush said, and—effortlessly, as if it were the most normal thing in the world—he played his role as a seller of lies. In 1992, Bill Clinton cited his opponent's phrase during the presidential campaign as an example of a broken promise, causing Bush to lose re-election. Just as Bill Clinton, the forty-second head of the American nation—during the scandalous *Zipper-gate/Tail-gate/Monica-gate*, with an innocent face of *It wasn't me*—swore not to have had sexual relations with Miss Monica Lewinsky (a White House intern) he announced the wonders of NAFTA, his own version of the snake's ointment: *This covenant means work. Good-paying jobs for the American people. If I didn't believe it, I wouldn't support this agreement.*

And so, it happened: the "beneficial" treaty caused the unemployment of hundreds of thousands of people, and the owners of small businesses went bankrupt. The well-paid jobs he spoke about were not intended for the workers, but for the big businessmen. The *bosses* opened their factories on the other side of the Rio Grande, the so-called "maquiladoras," where the Mexican day laborers, mainly peasants, did the same assembly work as the immigrants in the U.S. for a much lower wage and without the required demands of labor rights or health insurance. The agreement paved the way to get Latin American competitors out of the way and help the North American empire become the only export market to Mexico and Canada.

Larger-scale agricultural production required the use of herbicides, fertilizers, pesticides, and other processes worthy of a brilliantly sinister brain. A mango, an apple, a papaya, a chicken ceased to be simple fruits and poultry and became genetically modified organisms. Resentful, Mom would say eating them was the same as suicide. The agrochemical corporations that had already put their large part of the cake in their pockets announced that their fruits, vegetables, tubers, cows, and chickens were not only tastier and attractive, but healthier. "Look at this red, pulpy tomato, this sweet, seedless orange, this giant pumpkin, this cabbage, this cucumber . . . . They don't have bug bites like the ones Grandma grew in her yard," the propaganda read.

People's lives became just another business. What importance could one more or one less filthy person have? Where did all those crippled or brainless people who enriched the biotechnology industry come from? Monsanto had invaded the nation. One felt like crying upon seeing how cancer, obesity, autism, learning disabilities, and Alzheimers were taking over the population. Mom would (still) say that the United States had earned the right to be a world power; its imperialist measures were necessary to protect the values of democracy and freedom, as well as its economic interests. For her, the capitalist system was the best way to grow and advance. However, she wondered, "What do they want to achieve with so much greed and desire to fuck others over? Is it that the powerful can eat dollars?"

Mom commented that, at school in Ecuador, she met only one classmate who had trouble learning. "And in the school where I am now a teacher, it is difficult to find a kid who does not have a physical, emotional, or behavioral problem. Most regular students are no different from those classified as *learning disabled*."

In 2002, things got worse when China—responsible for feeding twenty percent of the world's population—along with other Asian countries, managed to avoid being left out of the game by invading many of the markets opened by one of those happy trade agreements. Imperial cities grew up shrouded in pollution and filth with the waste collected from textile, metallurgical and chemical factories. Mom was right to say it was scary to think about the future, to see that we advanced along with the garbage and the excrement. "Who will come after the Chinese?" she asked. "We will no longer have anywhere to run or anything to hold on to. The generations coming after us will need gas masks in order to breathe and survive. The planet will not have enough resources for eight or nine billion people starving to death. One crammed next to the other, poisoned with carbon monoxide, sulfur dioxide, plastic, and shit. I think it probable that the *zombies* in modern television series will materialize when there are no dogs, rats, and toads left, and we must eat each other. Cockroaches are rumored to survive even the detonation of an atomic bomb, but, as we go, not even they will make it. This general, imminent famine will render them extinct."

One of Mom's virtues, or flaws, depending on the situation, was to say, out loud, what she was thinking. She did not know what it meant to be prudent. This often got her into serious trouble. She repeatedly came home frightened and convinced that, the following day, she would be kicked out of the school where she had begun to teach. Listening to her, I couldn't help but wonder what ideas she would plant in the minds of the young people under her tutelage in the classrooms. She said that, as a civilization, we were screwed. There were too many dirty and dark games the planet and its inhabitants could no longer bear to which the powerful subjected us on a regular basis. "We are reaching that point in time when the only reasonable way to clear the atmosphere and relieve ourselves of the burden of eight or nine billion hungry wretches will be the use of a bomb. And not any bomb, like those threatened by crazy Korean dictator Kim Jong-un, but the mother of all bombs: the thermonuclear. That's when all the storytelling, foolishness, selfishness, and greed ends."

Mom says immigrants have always been seen as undesirable—therefore, persecuted. But with the factories and companies the *bosses* moved to Mexico, taking advantage of the free trade agreements, resentment and hatred increased. Immigrant workers ceased to be useful and became but a hindrance. The Immigration Department mobilized raids and processed large-scale deportations. Using buses, the agents picked up people in cinemas, restaurants, parks, stadiums, and all public places. There was nowhere to hide because *La Migra,* as the agents were called, were everywhere. They raided the businesses still standing and even showed up at the homes of the *illegals.* Mom was no exception. "The first time I escaped was because one of the coworkers in the *factory,* whose papers were in order, helped me get inside a box and put rolls of fabric on top of it. The twenty or twenty-five minutes the immigration agents spent there seemed to me like centuries. When that good man took me out of the box, I could barely breathe; and my legs were cramped. The second time, I remember someone shouting, *¡La Migra!* I ran like my life depended on it. I can't tell how I flew down the five floors separating me from freedom and then went on running for about ten blocks with these skinny legs, a six-month pregnant belly and cold as fuck."

The Immigration Reform signed by the fortieth President Ronald Reagan in November, 1986 legalized nearly three million undocumented immigrants who'd arrived in the United States before the first of January 1982. The amnesty allowed Mom to become a permanent resident, then a U.S. citizen. It also allowed her to own a textile business that she eventually lost in 1994 due to the Free Trade Agreement among the three northern countries. To Mom, Ronald Reagan was a god. She welcomed his decisions and mandates. His economic policies, called "Reaganomics," were the stuff of genius. During his two presidential terms, the economy saw a reduction in inflation. Ronald Reagan enacted cuts in domestic spending and lowered taxes. His talks with Soviet Secretary General Mikhail Gorbachev culminated in the 1987 Arms Control Treaty, which reduced the nuclear arsenal of both countries. Despite having increased military spending that contributed to tripling the federal debt, at the end of his eight years as head of state, Reagan obtained an approval rating of 68%, comparable to that received by Franklin Roosevelt at the end of his tenure.

For Mom, becoming a citizen of the United States meant having escaped a nightmare—she would no longer have to hide, no one could make her feel less, report her to the authorities, or deport her. Mom missed the country where she was born, longed for its wild nature, its mountains, its indigenous peoples . . . however, it was this New York, *where people were rude and insensitive,* that was the place she wanted to be.

Mom could not care less that many of her countrymen called her "sellout" or traitor. She was pleased to be a U.S. citizen. Mom knew historical facts that many U.S. natives took for granted or perhaps even ignored. When she said that Franklin Roosevelt was the only president elected four consecutive times, I had to look up the information to prove it was true. Indeed, Roosevelt died in April 1945—three months after being elected for the fourth time as Head of State. And yes, Franklin Roosevelt obtained an approval rating of 68% for his political-economic decisions in favor of the nation. Roosevelt led the country during the Great Depression, the time of the greatest economic crisis in U.S. history. The variety of programs and reforms included in *The New Deal*, the proposed plan to regulate the economy, brought relief and recovery to thirteen million unemployed and most of the banks that had closed their doors. In 1941, during his third presidential term, the Japanese attack on Pearl Harbor led to a declaration of war on Japan. In response,

Germany and Italy declared war on the United States. This is how the country formally participated in World War II. Under the leadership of Franklin Roosevelt, the United States became a superpower.

Mom says that when she arrived in the United States, she had to work at whatever odd jobs were available in order to eat and survive. "I couldn't aspire to anything better because I didn't have a professional degree or a trade, and I didn't speak the language." Nor could she afford to return: her mother had paid for a one-way plane ticket, so that, good or bad, she would have to find her own way. Her mother, the family, and everyone who knew her knew that in Ecuador she had no future and would always be a nobody.

Resentful, Mom told us the story:

"None of them had any trust in me. I was shy and insecure; and my physical attributes did not help me at all. I had a pair of gigantic tits, *Tremebunda size,* as my brother mocked me, which did not match the rest of my body. My breasts, as opposed to being an asset, were an atrocity, something grotesque, like the hump on Quasimodo's back—but in the front. To add insult to injury, I was mute. Talking was torture for me. I panicked, trembled, and tears were quick to threaten to come out whenever I had to speak. 'What nonsense is this silly girl going to come up with now?' Toby, my mother, would ask, cutting me off. She thought I was mentally challenged. She never changed her mind about it even when I was recognized by my teachers as a talented child and graduated from high school with honors.

"Determined to consider me an idiot, your grandmother most certainly thought all these recognitions were given to me out of pity. Toby was unhappy because she carried in her heart a secret—nailed like a poisoned thorn. The inexplicable thing was that she unloaded her bitterness only on me, not the other children."

Listening to the conversations Mom had with her siblings, I learned (much later, when old age was about to take my grandmother's life) that she confessed to the secret that poisoned her existence, that she had married a man she did not love and was forced to have unwanted children.

To this day, I can't explain why Mom had to pay the consequences of the rape and abuse Toby was subjected to during almost half her life by a certain Toby's damn degenerate stepfather. Mom also did not know why, but figured Toby suspected her of mixing 1080—rat poison—with the oatmeal our "supposed grandfather" ate in the afternoon. Since Toby was in charge of the kitchen, the children of the cursed Zacarías blamed her for wanting to kill the "*poor old man.*" They turned her life into a living hell. Another possibility, even worse, was perhaps that Toby thought Mom could be the biological daughter of that wretched man who continued to molest her—even after her marriage to my grandfather—under threats of talking about "the relationship" that, according to him, they'd both kept secret.

Fortunately, and thanks to DNA testing, so popular these days, that suspicion was proven false. Mom's father was Juan. My grandfather was known to have a certain preference for my Mom, but he could not do much in her favor because, as she said, unfortunately, in that house "the genius" had no voice or vote—his opinion was as good as poop.

Juan had ample knowledge of many interesting things. Some other things, well, he did not know much about. He was, however, always willing to make something up. All this knowledge, however, did not help him in the least. Success, for almost everyone, meant accumulating money and property. For Juan, knowledge was an inner pleasure, food for the neurons, joy of the spirit. To make a material profit from that which is incorporated into the brain, the spirit . . . never! Painfully, this world we live in, this attitude (viewed as laziness) is not forgiven. Those who do not produce and enrich themselves are simply losers.

The laws of genetics are demanding. Physical traits are inherited, and so is attitude, the way one sees things; and, since the damn genes do not forgive, here I am, condemned to accumulate information that, as Mom said, is absolutely fucking useless.

Mom celebrated this quality in my grandfather, but, in my case, she did not forgive me. When she looked at me, more often than not, her eyes showed disappointment. She thought I did not have the courage to be a winner. She figured I lacked ambition and was afraid of not being able to meet the expectations I had awakened in others—fear of not reaching the place they thought I should. According to Mom, my studies as an art historian and my tireless reading were a waste of time that would get me nowhere. At every opportunity, she'd recite the same lecture: "I came from a little shit country, not a pinch of English; however, I had a business, I completed university studies! And you, born in this great country, must go further."

She didn't accept my telling her that all I wanted was to be happy, to have time to enjoy my family, to do the things I liked and was interested in. Even if she didn't say it, for her, as for the rest of the world, success meant showing that you were up above the others; she wanted her children to be bill-fumbling pricks, even if they didn't know on what foot they stood. I didn't think of life this way. It pained me to witness people's ignorance. If anything, they recognized Einstein for his disheveled mane, Van Gogh for his severed ear, Washington because his face was on the dollar bills. If they had heard of Hitler, it was because of the repeated history about the thousands of Jews that, during the Second World War, the man had gassed in concentration camps.

If Mom heard Hitler's name, she would exclaim, "Crazy-ass man! Many called him the Antichrist because they saw in his actions the desire to destroy the loving labor of the historical Jesus. According to Nietzsche's work, *the Antichrist* was the perverse, priestly caste that used Christ's name to commit crimes and impose its will on those willing to accept its lies and abuse without resistance. Fernando Vallejo, copying from the Albigensians, rightly called the church of Rome *The Whore of Babylon*."

Malice and sarcasm were also traits Mom and I inherited from Juan. Mom was never shy to speak about the German monster, "If Hitler had tortured and eliminated those six million unhappy people, not by taking advantage of his privileged situation over the inferiority of others, but by appealing to the happiness promised by Christianity, surely no one would have condemned him or branded him a criminal. Just as they didn't the European conquerors who massacred, tortured, and raped thirty-six million Native Americans because, together with swords and horses, they brought along the cross and the Bible."

Mom resented that after all the humiliations that the native Americans, her ancestors, suffered at the hands of the Spanish, they continued to worship their culture. Mom told me that, during her trip to Spain with one of her friends, standing on the square in front of the cathedral of Santiago de Compostela, she felt as if she had been bitten by a viper.

"Our guide, a woman, pointing out one of three images, a disciple of Christ, said, 'The one in the middle represents Santiago the pilgrim; the one on the right, Santiago the Mata Moros (Moor killer); and the one on the left, Santiago the Mata Indio (Indian killer.)' At that moment, I saw blood flowing everywhere and heard cries of war from the Spaniards' throats as they charged to massacre the Indians: *'Santiago, get them!'*

"I could not contain my anger and, indifferent to the large number of people around me, I shouted, 'Santiago, son of a bitch! A whore gave birth to you! A thousand times, I curse you!' The guide, and those nearby, walked away, looking at me as one looks at some lunatic escaped from an asylum; and my friend, well, she ran toward the cathedral, pretending not to know me."

For me, that was Mom, the one who didn't mind making a fool of herself when it came to making her voice heard; the one who would make a fuss if someone tried to overwhelm her. I could not imagine her overshadowed and submissive as relatives say she was as a little girl. It is hard to believe that Mom was, at some point, naïve. Mom started studying architecture when the president of her country ordered the closure of schools and universities. This measure prevented students from gathering to plan and hold street demonstrations that jeopardized the government's dictatorial policy. That was when Mom came to the United States.

As she told it to us:

"My mother urged me, 'Go to New York to visit my sister *(The Whore)* for a couple of months before classes restart at the University.' I was happy to go with my cousins on vacation, unaware that Toby's real intention was to get rid of a burden: me.

"One less problem, one less mouth, one less fool.

"On the very second day of my United States visit, vacation ended. 'If you do not earn a living, you will starve to death, *you retarded piece of shit!*' sentenced *The Whore;* and I had no choice but to get into a factory. I worked on whatever I could: cutting threads off garments at the rate of a hundred heavy coats per hour, assembling fifty lamps a day, placing thousands of items on a conveyor belt to be bathed in gold, sealing in an oven the protective plastic for markers and pens. 'I am too intelligent to do shit like this,' I repeated to myself every other moment, seeing my hands sore and bleeding, aware that I was not a pack mule.

"For better or worse, my three sisters who remained in Ecuador all became doctors without daring the hell to which—

out of ignorance, anger, complexity, or necessity—my own mother had condemned me. Against wind and tide, I had to prove to myself, to Toby, and whoever dared question me, that I could get ahead, that I was not the failure they had predicted. Something told me it was not in my destiny to be a loser, that the life I was to live depended on me, that the best times would not come without my direct participation.

"I believed Shakespeare when he said: *Destiny shuffles the cards . . . but we are the players.* That's why, one day, I told myself: this is how far you'll come like this; enough of crying and lamentations! With the certificates in hand, the ones I'd brought from my country, I went to register at a university.

"The day I received my letter of acceptance from the City College of New York was one of the happiest of my life. I didn't know how I would afford my studies, but I would have a career even if it took me a lifetime to get it. I had gotten to that point.

I did not mind reaching into shit to get out of the life I was living."

Mom asked her old, wicked aunt for help—*The Whore*—still believing she could count on her, hoping it was possible to trust a snake. Mom was still young then and did not have enough experience or malice to know what to do in times of need, and just like that tale where a turtle helps a snake cross the river by carrying it on her back, Mom, like the turtle, believed that the creeping animal would not bite her.

"'Who do you think you are?' the old woman had said. 'We come to this country to break our backs like everyone else, not to study. *You retarded piece of shit*, just like your mother and your whole family of deadbeats.' I had no idea what she meant by that 'family of deadbeats' if she was Toby's sister. Without another word, she went to grab some papers out of a drawer and came back to brandish them in my face. I felt short of breath, like I was having a stroke. I cried with grief and anger. I couldn't pronounce a single word, dejected by a pain that squeezed my throat, when she said, 'This is the scholarship to study in the United States, which you applied to before you finished high school. I knew it would come to you, and I was waiting to steal it. And now I give it to you, *you retarded, book-eating piece of shit.*' The old woman possessed a sick, petty heart. She detested the spark of curiosity and desire for progress that we, Juan's children, had. Somehow, and with Toby's consent, I had come to this house where this damn woman tried to cut my wings, pull me down, so that I could not climb onto the lifeboat, but sink into mediocrity."

And Mom did nothing to avenge or punish the old, wicked aunt because that's what her parents had taught her: to endure abuse, mistreatment, without saying a word. Mom didn't even dare to tell her that her name wasn't "retarded piece of shit," as *The Whore* used to call her.

Years later, it was my sister Gilly, a thirteen-year-old girl, fed up with the abuses of the old woman, who took it upon herself to mete out justice, and kicked her out of our house like a filthy bitch: "You old shit, grab your things and get out of my house, or I swear on my mother's life I'll push you down the stairs," Gilly screamed, and *The Whore,* like the snake she was, spat her poison.

"Think you're brave, piece of shit, thick-lipped, ass-face? You're going to fry in hell next to your retarded mother," she said, clutching her vagina and showing Gilly her middle finger.

But she left, and Mom didn't say a word because that's what she had learned: to accept abuse without complaint.

Mom was full of fear back then. When my babysitter locked me in a closet for hours one time, I expected her to, at least, kick her ass, pull her by the hair, whatever, to this damn woman who was supposed to be taking care of me as a child under three years old. When Mom came to pick me up, I was unconscious and covered in my own piss and shit. Mom never left me with that scumbag again, but she didn't raise her voice either.

At some point, we all come up with evil things because it is what our nature dictates. But there are people like *The Whore*—miserable people—who are happy to do them. I'm thankful I ultimately grew up without her around. I would have grabbed her by the neck and kicked her out of our house for being such a bad person with Mom. Mom holds a grudge, says her guts twist when she remembers her, but accepts she was a necessary evil. "I now think it was all for the better because it made me observant, ready to harden my wings and fly. As my father said while we were planting the palm tree in front of our house (which, by the time I returned from the United States, would already be full of coconuts), 'Daughter, this plant needs nutrients, manure, cow poop . . . . Animal shit is the best fertilizer for plants to grow strong.' At that time, Juan and I did not know that this return of mine would take seventeen very long years."

Now, stuck in this traffic madness, as I slowly move along with the other drivers, I think about the times I told Mom I loved her. I told her many times as a child. I continued to love her, but I stopped saying it because her inconsistencies and attitude made me crazy. I loved her; nevertheless, I tried to make her feel guilty. I am both ungrateful and resentful; I just think of and remember the things that hurt me. I was never interested in knowing about her childhood or her adolescence. Mom didn't know how to ride a bike or skate. So, what were her games? What did she do when she wasn't going to school if, back then, there was no television, cell phones, or video games? Did she have friends?

She had them, or at least she had one because I remember Teresa—whose real name was Chiwon. Mom always mentioned having known her since the first grade, and then they graduated together in high school.

Teresa came to visit when I was starting elementary school and then when I was eleven. I remember her because she was Chinese, born in Canton, and cooked deliciously. Mom was happy with her visit. They laughed together at things that didn't make sense to me, like running out to the street during an earthquake, how tasty gooseberries were with salt on them, or the short skirts they hid under their demure uniforms. Listening to them, I learned they were fifteen when they first talked on the phone and had to spin the numbers with the tip of a finger inside a circular slot on a sort of flat, round rotor in order to dial. I know what those devices looked like because we had one at home until I was nine, when one day, all of a sudden, as if by magic, it was replaced by some one-piece cordless wonder with buttons.

Gilly told me it had been heartbreaking to see Mom mourn the death of her younger sister and, two days later, that of her friend Teresa, deaths and burials that she was not present for because her sister had died in Ecuador and her friend in California. The pain for those losses lasted for months. Ironically, she did not shed a single tear for any of her parents—although she always claimed to have loved Juan. "More than loving him, I admired his curiosity for the world around him and his crazy ideas. I would have liked to share more time with him, but Toby didn't let me. She said that women couldn't trust anyone, that men were evil and wanted to damage us. Even my father."

Grandpa worked for the intelligence department in the government military units that operated in Guayaquil. His job was to decipher secret codes hidden in international reports. Juan was a tomb with everything related to his work. He never divulged any secret information—he actually protected it. However, his discretion did not prevent him from making nasty comments about TV news reports. Mom says hearing about the events of the moment never seemed surprising to him.

"He was already a dead man. Now, his brother must be taken care of," he said as the whole world learned about the shooting of President Kennedy in Dallas. He also maliciously said, "It was obvious that Israel, with its 'Made in USA' fighter bombers, was going to annihilate Egyptian, Jordanian, and Syrian aircraft. Israel possesses air supremacy in Sinai because it has the United States wrapped around its little finger."

When the Apollo 11 moon landing was televised on July 20, 1969, and Neil Armstrong was seen inside his helmet and spacesuit, jumping over the lunar surface, Juan said, "Ha! Who is going to believe such a hoax? As if the gringos could reach the moon mounted on a broom!" That was one of the stories Mom told about Grandpa that made him seem crazy, but, for me, it made a lot of sense.

Once he was removed from his duties in the military offices, Grandpa devoted his time to "fooling around," as Grandma Toby said. He took notes in a logbook while attentively listening to the noises in the walls produced not by vehicle traffic but by the air's passage. According to him, since he was skilled at cracking codes, he could discover the secret messages sent by the spirits of those who had left this world.

"What were the results? Did he succeed?" I asked, and Mom responded, "I don't know. He began his quest the year I came to the United States, and, seventeen years later, when I returned home, they had thrown away all the old man's belongings."

There were so many things I didn't know about Mom's life—the reasons behind her being the way she was. It once crossed my mind that Mom had always been an adult. I never saw a picture of her before her arrival in the United States. Grandma Toby lived with us for three years, and I couldn't get to know more details because they talked to each other very little. Being mother and daughter did not mean much. They were a couple of strangers who did not know how to get along, either well or badly, and neither cared to learn anything about the other. I was eight years old when Toby came to our home. I was a child, but I realized that Grandma could not stand Mom, and rather resented her presence. Mom rightly said that to her mother, she mattered less than the dog. At least the little animal was nice, funny, and took care of the house—unlike her, her mother would say, who was "ugly, foolish, and useless as fuck."

Mom was probably the outcome of unfortunate intercourse: without desire or permission. I asked Grandma about Mom. "What was she like as a child? Was she naughty? What pranks did she do?" Grandma had nothing to say. She didn't even have the imagination to make up a story, put on a children's theater performance, and make me believe she loved my mom. It was all very sad.

I keep sluggishly rolling along with the traffic, feeling a sudden need to hug Mom and tell her I love her. As a teenager,

Mom and I watched a TV series whose name I don't remember. The show was about a stubborn old man. There was this episode in which the old man got entangled with his son in some situation and they were forced to spend time together—they maintained a distant and unfriendly relationship. Father and son conversed and discovered affinities they did not know they possessed. As the son said goodbye, the visibly-touched old man exclaimed, "I love you." Perhaps for the first time, the two men hugged and promised to say "I love you" to each other every time they met in case it was the last time they were together. At that moment, Mom and I promised to do the same; however, as time passed, I found it cheesy and, due to useless grudges, stopped doing it.

Feeling this sentimental surge running all over my body, I pull off the road and reach the corner of 21st Street and 41st Avenue in Long Island City, thinking about finding the old house where I was born. In its place, I find a building of luxurious apartments. Until early 2010, Long Island City was an industrial area where many buildings served as factories, and modest houses were located next to the Queensboro Bridge over the East River. On this side of the river, the silhouette of Manhattan was quite a spectacle. It looked like a postcard with the Empire State Building and a row of skyscrapers defying the heights. Today, Long Island City is a futuristic place in dramatic renovation with towers forty stories high, parks, and art galleries.

I get out of the car, walk into a bar, order a beer, and, as I drink, recall the front door of our house. The metal door was painted red. In front of it, in a photograph, Mom, a young woman, smiled with her two children. Mom held my hand and Gilly petted the little dog sitting on her lap. I remember that Gilly and I were happy living with her father until the moment *my* father came on the scene and things changed forever. I was seven years old when Mom told her then-husband that I was the son of another man. Gilly's father took it either as a gentleman or a coward. Who knows? Maybe he realized that was his opportunity to run away from the traitorous and disloyal woman Mom was. The fact is that the man grabbed his things and left. That is what Aldous Huxley called "cynical realism"—that is, the best excuse for an intelligent man to do anything in an intolerable situation. I still do not understand how Mom was able to handle that situation and emerge unscathed, without even a scratch, when others in the same condition ended up hairless, toothless, with broken bones, or even six feet under—with a neat hole in the middle of the forehead. I do not understand how I could accept that another man—an intruder—was my father and not the one I knew and who was by my side since I was born, *that* gentleman—who was good to me perhaps under the suspicion that there was something fishy in our whole father-son situation, given that we were visibly, and completely, different.

"Son, you must know the truth, even if it hurts. Gilly's father is not your dad," Mom said as if, instead, she was saying, "Get up, time for school" or "It's cloudy today." I don't think she realized that this "truth" made me sick and chilled my soul. Those words put an end to my innocence. They permeated my being with resentment, distrust, and cynicism. Since then, I knew that the purpose of life was to accumulate garbage—seeking perfection was in vain. Mom poisoned my life and, shit! My sister's, too.

Gilly hated this man with all her might. I hated him too, but, unable to change how things were, my sister and I had to master the art of simulation. We pretended to accept the unacceptable. I even hypocritically called him "Pa" when all I wanted was to kick his ass.

One time, getting him out of the way actually crossed my mind: I was willing to use a rodenticide, if necessary: the 1080 with which my Mom, supposedly, had poisoned Toby's stepfather.

Mom began to suffer episodes of vertigo that stopped me from carrying out the plan and destroying my life over that insignificant asshole. I don't understand how Mom could bear to live next to that worm who never loved or respected us, much less supported us. Luckily, one day, he disappeared from our lives again. I didn't know how the miracle happened, but it happened. I will not talk about him anymore—the motherfucker does not deserve the effort.

From the bar, I call my wife and tell her Mom is sick. "Gilly and her husband took her to the hospital." I tell her just so she knows. Mother-in-law and daughter-in-law maintained a relationship devoid of emotions, an icy relationship. There was no love or hate there. There was no tenderness, delicacy, animosity, none of that. When they spoke, there were no gestures; they looked like two statues that somehow had the freedom to move their lips. Fed up with how to deal with the two women who supposedly loved me, I asked Mom to be kind to my wife. "Do you want me to jump with pleasure when I see her? Be grateful that I am courteous to her and have resigned myself to seeing her as the woman you chose for your life," she said, grimacing angrily.

When I asked my wife to do her part and be cordial with Mom, her response was somewhat similar. "Should I jump with pleasure when I see her? Thank me for receiving her in our home and resigning myself to accept she is your mother." After that, I did not insist. Some prudent or wise man once said: "For mother-in-law and daughter-in-law to like each other, a donkey must climb a ladder first." He went on, "Mother-in-law and daughter-in-law: cats and dogs do not eat from the same dish."

With my daughters, the situation was different. Mom actually sat on the floor to play with them. She was not bothered by their screams and, if she saw them in trouble, she ran to help them. Surely, she sees in them my continuation or, more so, her own. When the first one was born, she took her in her arms and whispered, "Thank you for coming into our lives. With you, your ancestors are born again. I am in you; I am in your blood, in your genes."

Mom, as I always repeat, was a real nutcase—a mixture of foolishness and naïveté, she dreamed of finding a way to outwit death. For Mom, eternal life did exist. She knew of the conical pines that survived for more than five thousand years. She had read about a virus preserved in the Siberian steppes for thirty thousand years and brought back to life simply through warming up. Upon learning of the gigantic Galapagos tortoises, which exceeded five hundred years, she researched their diet and went for the fruits of cacti in an attempt to extend her life. Finally, the only thing she managed to do was line the walls of her stomach with the fruits' nuggets. If she never tried mercury pills—the alchemist elixir that three hundred years before the

Christian era was used by China's first emperor, Quin Shi Huang— it was because she knew for a fact they were poisonous. And since she didn't have any money, she couldn't aspire to the cryonic preservation process. Mom believed that she had biologically attained immortality through my daughters. Now Mom was in bed, fighting so that the part of eternity owed to her would not escape her.

After Gilly got married and went to live with her husband, Mom and I were both alone at home. During that time, Mom took her craft as a writer more seriously. She's thought that writing is another way to achieve eternity. In a book, the words of the writer live forever. After returning from her occupation as a teacher and finishing dinner, she would go to her bedroom to write and leave the door open. I never knew the reason, although I imagined it. Mom kept the doors of her room and the bathroom wide open because she was terrified of being locked up. Closing the doors meant being alone with herself, facing the voice of her conscience. "Confinement is for the mystics, for the blessed, and the monks. What kind of life is that? Appalling! Depressing! May the heavens free me from living in a cloister, in a monastery, in the mountains looking only at rocks and the sky! I would endure becoming Dracula and being locked in a gloomy castle only in exchange for immortality."

Mom used this logic as an excuse. Of course: she did not care how much her unusual habit and having to see her in the toilet fulfilling her biological needs bothered me. We know that a writer's craft requires solitude—I do not know if also silence. I don't know how Mom fulfilled those requirements because, even in those intimate moments when she, the writer, had to tear off her skin, bleed, and feel pain and fear, all along, she accompanied herself with noise and bustle. There were many times that, curious, I came on tiptoe to her room to see what she did until the wee hours of the morning, while listening to the howls of Mick Jagger, Jim Morrison, Eric Burdon,

Jeff Hanneman, and their fierce guitars and drums. I found her still, sitting in front of the computer. She looked like someone else, transfigured in the middle of the noise, and I wondered what ran through her mind. What was she writing? Next to her bed, she kept a trunk full of books. She read many authors, but always returned to Camus, to two books, in fact: *Caligula* and *The Myth of Sisyphus*. She repeated from memory certain lines found in those two volumes: "Men die and are not happy." "This world is of no importance and whoever recognizes this conquers their freedom." Sometimes, she read a few paragraphs out loud: "Many people think that a man suffers because, suddenly, Death snatches away the beloved woman. But their true suffering is less trivial; it comes from discovering that their pain doesn't last either. Pain, too, is just vanity."

But I was a teenager. I heard her babbling while thinking about video games and television series, about the more important things to *me*. Life, death, or freedom could not be compared to the horror of a troop trapped in a distant place populated by monsters in *Resident Evil,* or to the adventures of Shinji, the young man from the Japanese series *Evangelion.* At that young age, I didn't clearly understand the first thing about pain, wounds, and vanity . . . until I grew up and life kicked me in the ass. When you are a child, you look at what surrounds you, but you're not really seeing anything. When you grow older, you see yourself inside a Roman circus, in the arena, clueless and alone, and realize it's time to improvise, to use whatever weapons you may find at hand to defend yourself by attacking—because you don't want to end up mocked, broken, shattered . . .

Now a man, I understand the message from Mom's readings, the lessons she could not give me except through the words of others. I remember her voice, the deep intonation on the words as she read those lines. The memory of her voice saddens and touches me. I understand now. Of course, how could they not be her favorite books if she found in them her own way of seeing life? Sisyphus' punishment: using all his physical strength to push the heavy rock, bring it to the top of the mountain, just to watch it roll back downhill, and then having to repeat the task endlessly—a metaphor for the daily absurdity of our lives. Getting the heavy rock to the top meant a challenge, being able to outwit fate. However, it also meant discovering that happiness lasts just as long as that instant of joy—the fleeting ecstasy of achievement.

From the bar, I look at the building that stands where the old house once stood with its red metal gate and reminisce about those moments stored forever somewhere in my brain. I remember the times I found her asleep despite her unbearably loud music. I would turn off the light, the computer screen, the boom box, and let her rest in that position in which she felt comfortable and relaxed. With her body tilted this way or that, her legs collected, and her hands clasped under her head, struggling perhaps to escape from some bad dream. In those moments, I found her helpless. She looked like a little animal in need of affection. She stopped being the strong, cunning, and malicious woman; and all I wanted was to hug her, to protect her.

I don't know if I preferred her asleep or awake. Mom was a particular person, unique. She was a rebel, a madwoman, capable of any nonsense for the sole pleasure of showing that she could do it. Many times, my sister and I complained about not having a normal mother like all the other mothers. The mothers of our friends were regular people, without major complications. Women dedicated to taking care of their families and their children— their priority. Despite their occupations, they made time for other activities. They knew how to cook; they gardened, learned crafts, and took the time to attend meetings at their children's schools. Mom said these activities were not for her—she would place a finger in her mouth simulating nausea.

When we were teenagers and needed her more than ever, she used her love of literature as a pretext and joined a group of bohemians—instead of dedicating her time to her children and her home. Some of her friends were dirty vagabonds, drunks, and other fools who, like her, ran away from responsibilities and felt the urge to have a good time as often as possible. She had already left her youth behind, but that didn't stop her from keeping the bohemian alive.

I leave the bar and walk to the Long Island City piers under the Queensboro Bridge. Contemplating the towers that rise on the other side of the East River, I think rancor and resentment help one to remember certain moments. One remembers them to prevent time from reducing their intensity even when aware that they hurt our souls. "Mom, you always complained about your mother's indifference and lack of attention. However, you did the same to your children. I am disappointed in you. I am hurt. Bitterness squeezes my chest. I do not forgive your abandonment, your detachment. Oh Mom, until the end of your days you will be this selfish, irresponsible woman, unable to love! Mom, in spite of it all, I love you. I love you, even if I never tell you again. Mom I know I'm doomed to love you forever."

"There is a disease that hides in the blood, in the heart, in the neurons. When it attacks, this ailment weakens reason and idiotizes a person to the point of leading them to place the well-being of someone else before their own. This ailment, commonly called *love*, is so powerful it can even force the afflicted person to kill anyone who hurts or harms the loved one. I thought I would never suffer such a disorder, let alone be infected twice. Seeing another flesh come out of my flesh clouded my understanding. I fell prey to a spell and forgot that I was the most important thing in life." You wrote that once, referring to your feelings for me and my brother Adrian. Now that I read these words, I understand why you have always forgiven my outbursts and my tantrums. Today I understand your motives and even if you didn't say it, I have felt your love and know it is forever.

I think of Mom as I order a martini and my husband a bottle of Pellegrino water. We are in a beachside bar, in front of the hospital where we brought Mom after finding her disheveled on the bed. When I saw her, I thought she was dead. I felt my heart churn. I love this woman life gave me as a mother—although I didn't always let her know. I learned to love her as I discovered, with her, the difficult art of living. There was a time when Mom lost her business, her house, and the things we were used to. Mom had a degree that accredited her as a mechanical engineer; however, she could not get a job because, due to recent technological advances, the skills she'd learned years before had become obsolete. We moved into a small apartment and, to survive, Mom had to work in a supermarket. I couldn't stand to see her collapsed, fragile, unprotected . . . she, who always showed herself to be the strong one, the one who faced adversity without complaints and boasted of not knowing what fear was. I never wanted to see her like this. I preferred her defiant as a fighting cock, ready to stick her finger in anyone's eye who came to cross her.

There was a lump in my throat. I felt my soul slip out of my body and I burst into tears. Jack, always so practical, with no time to waste, called 911. My husband and I had gone to visit her at her apartment where, according to her complaints, she was under "house arrest"—to which I had sentenced her. Some house arrest that was. She escaped whenever she wanted. Even planned a trip with the new friends she'd made in Florida—bizarre slackers who called themselves poets because they had no trade. She didn't care that Jack and I warned her about the dangers of Cuba where freedom and the rights of its citizens were not respected. She grabbed her suitcase and went away with her writer friends—the Colombian Palonino and the Chilean Oregón—to Castro's Island to eat cats. She herself told us that, in Cuba, no one really knew what kind of meat they put in their mouths. "There was very little left for the people after the revolution and the embargo."

In a photograph, she showed the only cow she saw on the island. The animal was strapped to a pole as an exhibit so that people (especially children) would know what a cow was. "Gentlemen, let's delight ourselves with a tasty cat in sauce, drink a lot of rum to endure these bad times, and then, of course, let's smoke a cigar," they were told by one of the other Cuban writers, the ones who welcomed them to the island.

My husband assured me that Mom was lying. He could not believe "the *mama,*" he said, because one could never tell how much of what she said was true and how much an invention of her magnificent imagination. The truth was that we knew she was back from Cuba but had not returned to her apartment. A day later, I, dying of anguish, asked Jack to accompany me to pick her up. Mom had settled in the house of the Colombian poet and how at ease she was when she came out to receive us in her pajamas. No matter where she went—Greece, Costa Rica, Peru, Spain, Mexico, Russia (we saw a photo of her in Moscow surrounded by strangers, "celebrating life," as she called her getaways)—the problem was that we only found out about it either from other people or when she was finally back.

Mom was a free woman. She could do with her life whatever she wanted. What bothered us was her selfishness, her lack of consideration for her children; something bad could happen to her and we would not know where to go, either to help her or to collect her bones.

I had turned eighteen when my mom, "the gypsy," went for three months to the Dominican Republic, leaving my brother of only twelve years in my care. How could a mother play with the safety of her children like that? She needed to complete a few courses to get a master's degree and earn more money—that was her excuse. And that was, as always, the full extent of the matter: no further analysis. No debate.

It never occurred to her to think of the dangers two kids all alone out here could face. We could have suffered an accident, caused a fire, fallen into the hands of a bully, a kidnapper, a sexually-ill person . . . any *human* rat and it'd be goodbye, little doves. Happily, my brother and I were not fools or crazy fantasists, we knew we could not trust anything or anyone who came to us with kisses, gifts, and sweet words to leave us skewered like meat on a stick.

Mom's siblings passed judgment on everything without having the slightest fucking idea of what they were talking about. According to them, children raised in the United States did not know respect and were ignorant. They dared to judge us because they did not know that, in school, from an early age, teachers taught us to recognize abuse, to defend our rights, to be self-sufficient, and to avoid what could harm or compromise us.

According to my aunt and my uncle, Adrian and I were not as well-educated as their children, our cousins—kids who came from countries where good manners, courtesy, and obedience were still preserved. They did not realize they were raising hypocrites who would hide their true personalities under ornaments and traditions. What fucking idiots. In addition to being pretentious and self-conscious, they had the obligation to obey and satisfy half the world with that stupid "*mandé*" ("Tell me what to do!") and their culture of respect: I respect, you respect, we all respect. Respectful repressed dudes who were frightened and did not know where to go when reality stopped them head-on. To them, my brother and I were the *Simpsons* and also the *Beavis and Buttheads:* rude, rebellious, violent kids who did not know how to use the three forks and four spoons on the table, who did not know all the breeds of dogs or the names of kings, princes, and their royal entanglements.

But, back to the topic. Mom came from that culture of obedience, fear, and respect. Back then, Mom hesitated to make a comment for fear of offending someone. Shouting was for her an outburst, and insults, a lack of modesty. What the hell had they done to my poor mom? *Good manners* had her fucked up and mentally castrated! I did not devote myself to the study of art, history, and all those activities important to Adrian. It was enough for me to flip through one of his books to enjoy the works of art or inform myself of certain facts without trying to delve into any subject like my brother did. On one of those pages, I read how the taboos about sex that Christianity dragged from Jewish beliefs and St. Paul's rejection of sexual union created a damning idea of the body, nudity, and sex. For the mentality of medieval man, the body was a filthy receptacle of diseases and vices; the flesh was weak, temporary, and condemned to die. So, the nudes then depicted were ugly, awkward, and far from any sexual intention. The Renaissance brought back the ideals of beauty found in classical antiquity, legitimizing a new vision of something alive, noble, and magnificent, as nudity was. Eroticism was present; from idealized representations, it transitioned to other styles of a palpable carnality. In *The Last Judgment*, the great variety of naked bodies burned by the flames of hell was scandalous. This caused Pope Pius IV to order fabric to be painted to conceal the genitalia of the figures painted by Michelangelo. I could imagine the stupor and repulsion of the clergy, of medieval men—and even some repressed men of the present faced with works like *La Maja Desnuda (The Naked Maja)* or *The Origin of the World.* Goya and Courbet could be burned alive for painting the naked female body with such unprecedented and scandalous veracity, gloriously showing the genitals surrounded by pubic hair. In these works of art, reality is imposed in a brutal way and the viewer can hardly escape from it. That reading made me see Mom as a beautiful and true human figure, sculpted with virtues and defects, owner of a rebellious, contradictory, and indomitable spirit that good manners and blind respect tried to control and destroy. With luck, little by little, the disappointments, frustrations, and tremendous blows life deals us all steadily removed the layers of meekness, passivity, and conformism that hid her true self.

The final trigger to her freedom from that lethargy, I am convinced, was my accusations—legitimate—of the perverse intentions of two damn men. I refused to visit the house of my father's friend and his wife. Horrible things were happening there that out of shame I didn't dare to tell anyone. When we were left alone, my father's friend caressed me in a way that made me feel dirty. "I don't want to go to that house, I don't want to go to that house," I complained and, incredibly, my parents couldn't read the fear in my protests and tears. Mom still could not discover the evil hidden behind their good manners. She thought the beautiful gifts from that man were a sign of affection when he was actually looking for ways to strip me of my self-love and crush me like a cockroach. Mom took those smiles and flattery as sincere signs of friendship when what that hyena wanted was to move smoothly until he reached the victim and left us to drown in his shit.

One morning, the rat called to announce that he would come to visit. Mom happily passed me the phone to greet him and it was then, trembling with fear, that I quoted his exact, horrible words, "This man is asking me that, when we are alone, I let him see the hairs growing between my legs." Dad paled when he discovered how, in front of his eyes, his childhood friend's good-natured, good-hearted disguise fell off. This was the man he had chosen to be my godfather! With amazement first and then with incomparable disgust, Mom woke up to the garbage around her, the rot hidden by people she believed could be trusted. At that moment, I clearly heard a roar, a growl equal to that of the tiger in the zoo. Mom turned into a monster, took the phone, and screamed: "You goddamn motherfucker, I'm going to your house right now to kick the shit out of you." Dad, still in shock, refused to believe what was happening, the damage that beast had planned. Mom said, "If you don't want to go, it's okay; stay stupid! Don't defend your daughter! I'm going to kill that motherfucker!"

But the coward had run away. He left his wife behind, unaware of the circumstances. We never heard from him again, but Mom, as a precaution, and to fulfill her revenge, *kept a pocketknife* in her handbag to use if the rat ever crossed her path again. From that day on, Mom stopped being the "shitty retard," as her aunt called her, who endured all the shit thrown at her without rebelling.

My dad was a good, quiet guy, but those weren't the qualities Mom needed in a man. Dad didn't intend to go anywhere in life; he lacked will and character. He was a poor little lamb. Befitting his luck, he was not able to lift a finger to change the course of things. He showed no desire to light a fire or burn. My father obeyed Mom's orders without questions or opinions of his own as if opening his mouth cost him a great effort. I loved Dad. I often think of him—the moments that will never leave because I have them stored inside, always about to burst out of my chest. I feel like crying, I sob, I close my eyes and remember when, in the afternoons, I expected him to arrive from work to go for a walk, clutching his hand or going around the neighborhood riding our bikes. On Sundays, Dad would wake me up early, and, while I took a shower, he would make boiled eggs, bacon, and pancakes—these were part of the special breakfast on weekends. At eleven o'clock in the morning, we were ready to go for a walk. We took my brother with us so that he would not start crying. We went to the animal farm, our favorite place in Flushing Park. We fed the chickens, watched the ducks swim in a huge lagoon, rode a cart pulled by horses, and, after hamburgers and fries, went spinning in the carrousel until it was time to close the park.

I think Mom hated those walks. The times she accompanied us could be counted with the fingers of a single hand. Those moments ended though. The animal farm and the carrousel were left in the past. These places, I don't even know if they still exist. Mom decided to break that bond, which, for her, was never a serious commitment, but something trivial that helped her fight her weariness. For Mom, a man was useful if he could cover the expenses and allow her time to study. What Mom needed was someone to lean on, build momentum and jump forward. Mom was not willing for another second to live with a good and quiet guy (who made her mad), and just as she changed her clothes every morning, she replaced him with another man.

This new man was a scumbag with a villain's face and airs of grandeur who believed himself an irresistible male. I don't know what Mom was thinking when she got involved with that rat. Maybe Mom still felt insecure, doubted her worth as a woman, as a person, and clung to a body that was nothing but a body full of shit. According to comments from Lily, Mom's sister, the guy met her when Mom was pregnant with me. That scoundrel gave no fucks that the woman was pregnant with another man's child.

Back then, Mom had huge tits (years later *they* were cosmetically reduced) and surely the size of those tits drove the pig crazy. It disgusts me to remember that guy. It makes me angry to know he fathered my brother while Mom was still living with my father. So many years wanting to forget that detail, drive it out of my mind, and pretend it never happened. That miserable man was so shitty that he wasn't even moved by his own son. "Can't you see he is your son?" I can imagine Mom's voice demanding the pig be a father to my brother, to pay attention to him, to offer him a little affection.

He hated me. He called me "the devil's spawn." He said I was an ugly, skinny, disrespectful, thick-lipped little girl. If he didn't assault me, it was only because he knew I would tell my dad, and my dad—"the asshole," as this guy had nicknamed him— had him warned.

On the Hispanic channel, there used to be an ad for a law firm that said something like, "If you've been hit by a car, pushed across the street, pulled off a train, fallen from a building, slipped on wet pavement, rolled down stairs, or suffered any other mishap, call 212-CANTAZO. You can receive thousands of dollars more than with other attorneys . . ." or some such. "Remember, in case of accidents, dial 212-CANTAZO." I took advantage of that commercial to make the pig rage. One wrong stare from him was enough for me to shout, "In case of accident, call 212-CANTAZO!"

And so, in that "push and pull" of tantrums and desires to kill, time passed. I could never accept the presence of the undesirable one. For me, it was impossible to get used to something I couldn't stand: the theater, the staged deception of an actor cajoling his only spectator; and Mom flattering him, making him believe he was charming. I was disgusted to see Mom and the pig hold hands as if they were a couple of lovebirds. Yet the most unpleasant thing of all was to hear them in the bedroom as they whispered and laughed at the noises of the bed.

He did not care about his son. Because of his damn lack of interest, my brother became a sullen and resentful child. However, thinking himself funny, the pig would wrap his arms around Mom's shoulders and mine as if we were Daddy, Mommy, and the beloved little daughter. From a pig, the only thing one can ever expect is pig's shit.

Overnight, so to say, the pig started to swap insults for beautiful words. I stopped being the ugly, skinny, and reckless girl and became "the little princess." He did not deceive me with his attentions though. He was looking for something. I always had a good nose for scumbags—there's a reason I became a cop. My soft body took on sinuously provocative shapes, my legs filled my pants, and my breasts bulged in my blouses. I went from a thick-lipped little girl to a woman with a sensual mouth in virtually no time.

I know that, to Mom, I was still a girl. Still am, probably. However, I do not know if she sinned by acting naïve or if the pig had her fooled—or threatened—because she could not see the obvious. The guy was staring at me all over the house, especially when I came out of the shower with my hair wet. I put Mom on alert, "Why doesn't your boyfriend go to work in the mornings? Instead, he parks the car a block from the house to wait to take me to school." My question angered her for a moment. I saw doubt cross her eyes; but then, calmly, she asked, "Daughter, are you sure of what you are saying?" My complaints were legitimate, even if they seemed like revenge or a strategy to get that damn intruder out of the way.

The next morning, Mom left breakfast ready on the table for my brother and me. "I'll be back right away; going to the corner grocery store to get bread and jam. When I come back, I want to find you ready for school." She lied. All shopping was done on the weekends and the bag of bread and the jar of fresh jam were on the table. Mom returned fifteen minutes later empty-handed, stood next to me, and stroked my hair with a tenderness I had not discovered in her before. Mom loved us, but she didn't know how to show her feelings. She barely talked to us to ask how we were doing at school and didn't check our homework or play with us. It seems to me that her attitude was the product of the harshness and detachment with which her mother treated her. For a while, Grandma lived with us. She and I came to love each other, to get along, but that did not mean my grandmother wasn't a piece of shit with her own daughter. It was Grandma who taught Mom that contact between people was not good: no pampering, tenderness, hugs, or kisses.

At that moment, feeling her caresses in my hair, I was moved, and embraced her with all the strength I was capable of. I was considered a rebellious and rude girl, willing to do any silly thing to make Mom angry.

That's why to challenge and punish her, I wore miniskirts, loose blouses, and, as if I were a vulgar madwoman, painted my eyes black, my mouth red, and went out to my friend's house. She could think whatever she wanted about my behavior; she could threaten to slap me or send me to live with my paternal grandmother . . . I just didn't plan to tell her where I was going. Mom never knew that, as soon as I reached the corner of our street, I took off my makeup and put on the leather jacket I kept hidden in my backpack. I would come back at eleven o'clock at night smelling like cigarettes. I'm not going to lie: my friend and I learned to smoke while locked in her bedroom with the windows open so that her mom wouldn't discover us. We would smoke while we did our homework and watch TV. Mom kept some of her threats: she would wait for me at the door and slap the shit out of me. I shouted that I hated her, that I couldn't stand her, and that, the next time she hit me, I wouldn't come back home. All those bad feelings and grudges were undone by her hand rubbing my head.

I do not know where Mom went, what she did, or what happened during those fifteen minutes she was out. The truth is she returned a different person: smiling, relieved, as if she had gotten rid of a shackle or a weight that prevented her from acting freely. Something happened in those fifteen minutes because the guy did not talk to me ever again nor did he wait for me in the car. Sometime later, we no longer found his things in the house. We didn't see him again; it was as if he had evaporated into the thin air. Mom did not give us an explanation. My brother and I did not ask questions either. We closed then and there on that episode in our lives when, unfortunately, the cause of our misery was my brother's father.

Poor Adrian! Some time ago, he confessed to me that he had turned to a psychologist to help him erase that lack of maternal interest and care, and the selfish behavior of a father who never knew how to act the part. Perhaps that is why my brother married a judicious, dedicated, reliable woman, always attentive to her family, who never put her well-being before that of her husband and daughters. In other words, a very different woman from Mom. Maybe that's why I chose Jack, a man who is not afraid to express his feelings, who screams when something bothers him, who laughs out loud when happy, and kisses me when he needs to. Jack is a man concerned with being happy and making me feel happy. When Mom was free of that rat, her life changed. She resumed her writing, and started meeting with friends and having fun at parties and in crowds. Not interested in meeting or starting a relationship with anyone, Mom had discovered that the man she was looking for, and needed, did not exist.

I drink my second martini as I watch the waves on the coast ebb and flow. The sun shines on the water. The sand is a white sheet embroidered with tiny diamonds flashing under the light. Seagulls flutter and, on the fly, pick up pieces of bread or chips that children throw into the air. The landscape is beautiful—a view nature gifts us to the delight of our senses. However, I feel like something alien stands before my eyes—something my gaze crashes against, leaving me indifferent. Sadness manages to take me out of the world; it scares me to think about losing that woman I love, because I might regret it. Melancholy suffocates me: that feeling of silence and emptiness hurts. Mom is part of my story, of my person. If she dies, I will be incomplete. As if one of my senses were stripped off me. As if someone snatched the air I breathe or a chunk of my soul. We are not always together, but hearing, from time to time, her voice on the phone and knowing she's alive is enough to feel her presence. Adrian insists on saying Mom and I never finished cutting the umbilical cord. Maybe he is right—or whatever—because by a certain sensorial, emotional, or physiological mechanism, Mom hurts somewhere in *my* body, in *my* heart, in *my* blood.

I feel my husband's embrace, wanting to protect me from the pain, and I remember the first time I saw Mom sick. My brother had to take care of her because I was not able to see her in that state—much less think that we could lose her. Mom was not affectionate. She was not a mother watching every step we took. Rather, she was indifferent, dry. On very few occasions, she hugged us or kissed our cheeks tenderly. Her feeble ability to express her feelings was both odd and touching. She had to get old, and suffer disappointments and goodbyes, to get rid of resentments (especially with her mother) and be able to say freely, "I love you, Son; I love you, Daughter."

Mom began to suffer from vertigo. The episodes, quite frequent at first, were so strong and long-lasting that they paralyzed her. Unable to control the dizziness, there were many times she lost her balance and fell to the floor. Fear of passing out and thinking death was haunting her caused Mom to enter horrendous depressive states.

Having been educated in a religious school, it seems like the nuns did not do a good job as they failed to get Mom to believe in saviors, virginal women, miracles, and promises of eternal life. For her, religious teachings were tales of loonies disguised as prophets and messiahs whose mission was to deceive the poor in spirit. "One must be really stupid not to realize one is just a part of the disorder, of the crazy chaos, full of useless galaxies in an absurd, indifferent universe. One must be crazy to believe that flesh and blood beings, genetically selfish, predisposed to envy, revenge, and harm, can be holy and, after death, will live eternally happy. 'Do not be afraid,' they tell you, 'you will die and then you will have a long and happy life; you will enjoy everything you did not have in life. You will reach paradise.' Lies, all these are stories to safeguard you from the horror of dying. Misleading words, so that you can endure the injustices of life without complaining."

For a while, the subject of death upset Mom. She could not speak of the end without its horror making her wail, "Do not expect me to die quietly in my bed as if I were a miserable dog. I am going to kick and scream. Death is an injustice, a damn absurdity." Over the years, Mom learned, like everyone else, to live with this horror as best she could. She eventually lost her fear of death—but never her contempt for that inexorable moment when one ceases to be a person to become an infamous mass, to become part of the nothingness. Quite cheesy and dramatic, Mom requested that, at her wake, we play a song from her homeland that goes: *I want to be buried like my ancestors, in the dark and fresh belly of a clay pot.*

Mom was convinced that, after she died, it would all be over. Nothing holds value for the dead: not air, not love, not the most wonderful of memories. However, she was against cremation. She considered it a repugnant act, a lack of respect for a body that was the vessel of the mysterious power that was life. I mocked her by saying whatever happened to her remains would no longer be her business and cremation was cheaper than a burial. Her answer was that she didn't care that existence sucked, that it was crap to be left behind. "Life, with its torments, horrors, and fears, is an opportunity for those fortunate enough to be born. It is a pity that one should get it only to turn into ashes. You bury me whole, so my eyes, my heart, my guts . . . slowly decompose and transform into another kind of life. I want to continue to be alive."

Mom thought music was necessary at the moment of departing toward the unknown and leaving the bereaved behind to reflect on how fleeting life was, how useless it was to want to cling to it. After reading *Deutsches Requiem*, a short story by Jorge Luis Borges (Borges' little books were scattered all over the house) she decided that "The Clay Pot" no longer suited her, that Brahms' *German Requiem* would be perfect for that moment of her journey to another world, the one my atheist brother called "the journey to nowhere." I didn't read the story, but there was no need because Mom talked all the time about that masterpiece, the story about the commander of a Nazi concentration camp, prosecuted and convicted for the crimes committed by him and Nazi Germany against humanity. While waiting for the moment to confront the firing squad, the Nazi rambled on about his inhuman behavior, feeling no fear or pity for the victims, firmly believing that the world of the future should be governed by "violence and faith in the sword." Convinced of the ideals of the Nazi party, the commander expressed hope that if glory was not for Nazi Germany, it could be for other nations: *Let heaven exist even though our place is in hell.* For Mom the story of the commander was fascinating: her eyes shone as she gave details about the facts she had found out about the nefarious character.

After the moments of euphoria she enjoyed with this cruel and depressing tale, Mom changed her mind yet again, now believing it better if the final journey—of which she spoke as if the dead were someone else—were fun. "No weeping and wailing, no funeral marches, no sacred words, final judgments, Brahms, Bach, or Chopin. I want joyful music for the people who accompany me in that moment of my 'transubstantiation' because music is for them, for the living. What could be better than rock-and-roll?"

It was then that Mom became passionate about Maroon 5 and Adam Levine. "*Moves Like Jagger* wasn't bad at all," she said. She loved that song and even chose to dance to it with my brother on his wedding day. Adrian had asked Mom to choose a song she felt united them. I think Mom chose well: that song managed to unite them because my brother was happy. He laughed as he and Mom mimicked Mick Jagger's dance moves: *I don't need to try to control you / Look into my eyes and I'll own you with them / moves like Jagger / I've got the moves like Jagger / I've got the moves like Jagger*. This was, for Mom, music made to feel happy, to feel alive—and perfect for the final farewell.

Mom could not stand the screams of the opera singers nor did she appreciate melodies that squeezed the heart and strangled the soul, such as funeral marches. She did not pretend to have exquisite taste or to be refined enough to endure the pleading underlying such music. *Brahms' Deutsches Requiem* became creepy and, even more so, *Mozart's Requiem*. Risking (but not caring) she might be labeled as irreverent, she said this music did not feel sublime— even less so, knowing the *Requiem* had been written by a dying man. It is said that Mozart was seriously ill when he wrote it and could not finish it. Speaking of that sacred music, Mom told us the first time she visited the medieval castle called *The Cloisters* in Upper Manhattan, she was about to scream in anguish and leave the place, horrified. It was eleven o'clock in the morning when they opened the doors to visitors and she realized she was the only one there to climb the stone stairs at the entrance to the building. "Through the speakers, one could hear, like whispers, the

Gregorian chants—the same liturgical music the nuns played during Mass in the school chapel in my country. The nuns said this was the most beautiful music ever produced by man: listening to it purified the soul and connected the human being with God. I claimed otherwise. Just like when I was a little girl, at that moment, listening to those Gregorian chants, I felt I was headed for the afterlife. My skin bristled, anguish settled in my throat, suffocating me—and, believing I'd heard the cry of my teacher condemning me to hell for my heresy, I shouted, '*Holy shit!*' Just as I was ready to run downstairs, I saw other people entering the monastery and that calmed me down."

After hearing that story, I wanted to know what heresy she talked about. Why did the nuns send her to hell? Through laughter, Mom answered, "I asked them what the sixth commandment meant by 'Do not fornicate.' To avoid the subject, one nun said it was a verb that indicated an action similar to lying or stealing. When in grammar class they asked me to conjugate a regular verb, I said: 'I fornicate, you fornicate, he fornicates . . .'"

Jack gets up and tenderly kisses me on the forehead. He asks if I want something to eat and I say no. He takes a seat by my side. I would like to be alone, but Jack insists on accompanying me in these sad moments. *Mom will come out of this test triumphant as she has always done. Mom can't die*, I think as I watch Jack drink his Pellegrino. Jack has his stuff, his tricks, his own tastes, and I respect them. He is proud of his Italian or, rather, Sicilian origin; that's why Mom called him Rambo, Al Capone, or Don Corleone. Jack does not drink alcohol or do drugs—he does not allow any harmful substance to alter the proper functioning of his mental activity. Jack worked as a detective in the New York City Police Department for twenty years. For him, a healthy, agile, sharp mind is the most important tool of the trade. It keeps him alert and allows him to focus on the smallest details of what may be wrong. Although a few months ago he was removed from his position, he has not stopped being a policeman. My husband is an innate detective. He is skilled at fishing out and unraveling whatever he wants to know about people while talking to them. What for most people are unimportant things, words, and gestures (which generally go unnoticed), for his eagle eyes are clues that lead to guilt and deception.

Mama, as Jack calls Mom, confessed to me that she did not know what this "Italian rattle" who is my husband did to make her fall into the lie, but she preferred to be struck by lightning and fall dead a thousand times rather than admit that she was snooping around the papers that her son-in-law kept in a desk drawer, or that, just for the pleasure of hearing him scream, she threw the box of *cannoli* in the trash, or that she tangled up the fishing line on his fishing rod. It makes me laugh to see Mom, at barely five feet tall, confront my husband and shout, "Think twice before you mess with me and accuse me of something I've never done, something which hasn't even crossed my mind!"

His tricks and deductive methods (his eagle eye) don't work with me because, well, I just tell him to go to hell. There's a reason why I was a criminal investigator in the police department where we met. He knows very well that I have a license to carry weapons and that my hand does not tremble to unload a couple of bullets if the occasion requires it.

I gulp the Martini down and order another. The liquor helps me to relax. More than anything, it helps to appease this pain stuck in my chest ever since I found Mom lying in bed as if she were dying. I finish the second Martini and ask Jack if we can go home so I can rest for a moment. The car glides down the road, lined with both natural and man-made lagoons that surround hundreds of pretty homes painted in flamingo pink, terracotta, and olive green— the colors of South Florida. The air conditioner, at full blast, suffocates me. I turn it off, ignoring Jack's immediate complaints: "I'm drowning. I am sweating here. See? My eyes are clouded." Through the window, the wind feels heavy, wet, and sticky. One can feel the ninety-degree heat the meteorologists announced for today. It smells of the sea, sun, and burnt leaves; my thoughts return to Mom. There was something inside of her that prevented her from taking care of a house, from having a home. *Mom, you really made us suffer from your instability!*

I often wondered why we went, like gypsies, from one house to the next, and not one ever managed to get her to settle down. Mom owned a house and an apartment, but we didn't stay in them for long either. One spring, across from our apartment in Long Island City, a group of Romanian gypsies moved in. The house they occupied was large enough for the five adults and six children who made up the family, yet they slept outside, in a rickety truck parked on the side of the house where the sky was their roof. Dressed in skirts and blankets, rings and bracelets, the women placed a table and an awning next to the door and there they sold colored candles, amulets, and tarot cards. They also read palms. Mom admired their way of being, their dressing style, their music, and lightheartedness, and, if allowed, would have joined the group and dragged my brother and me into that life. Happily, she could not make friends with these people because only one of the women spoke English. Since then, *Gypsy* was the nickname I gave her.

One day, Adrian and I found her looking, as if hypnotized, at a graphic in one of my brother's art books. "That impressive work is called *Christina's World*," Adrian said. I looked at the painting: a woman was crawling on the grass. "Poor woman abandoned on the road; though wounded and torn to shreds, one day she will arrive at that house on the horizon," Mom said in a trembling voice.

"Christina was Andrew Wyeth's neighbor," Adrian explained. "The artist expressed his own pain in painting that woman's agonizing crawl through the countryside. Christina was not abandoned, she was crippled."

"You can be crippled without being a paralytic," said Mom, with pain in her voice, and I understood then why we went from one house to the next. Unconsciously, Mom wanted to return to the house (her parents' house) from where, according to her, she was evicted and made to feel crippled. She knew she would never return; it was not possible because there was nothing left of the things that were dear to her. Her parents had separated, her siblings were gone, and her dogs had died. That house no longer existed.

"It is inexplicable," I tell myself, "there are seemingly banal facts that carry no importance to anyone. Nevertheless, they touch someone and their effects accompany that person for the rest of their life." Time passes, people die, and the world could explode, yet that fact, which was cause for resentment, continues to poison that person's soul. "How stupid human nature is!

Mom, so strong and brave, was unable to tear off the damn feeling of rejection that did not let her live in peace or, at least, relieve her of the grudge . . . the grudge against whom? Her own mother, or the memory of something else thought to have been left in the past?"

Swapping places left and right, we came to live in an apartment in Elmhurst, a neighborhood near Jackson Heights. This neighborhood was known as "Chapinerito" or "Cali York" because there lived "the lords of the white goddess": chiefs of the Cali cartel. Mom befriended a couple of lazy Colombians whom she claimed she envied because they were free: they (living on the streets) didn't have to worry about having a roof or anything. Poor Mom, she talked so much crap: she had no idea about the hardships the *homeless* go through. On Saturday morning, Mom would meet her *parces* on the sidewalk outside the McDonalds at 82nd St. and Roosevelt Avenue. Mom said what happened in those streets and the stories of "the mono Arcila" and "the paisa Ospina" inspired her to write. With them, she learned to recognize both the undercover police and the capos who, like any other Colombian, ate at *Little Colombia,* a popular restaurant.

"Look, those are Alex Barrera and 'El Patrón,' Evelio Romero. The one crossing the street is Arizabaleta. We all know who they are, except the police. We love these bosses. They give '*platica*' to everyone in the neighborhood and no one snitches on them. Whoever dares, though, must know someone will bring them *chumbimba,* and goodbye life." Mom says her homeless pals warned her whenever the capos walked past them on their way to their *businesses* or to buy *Bono* (bread)from *La Abundancia Bakery.* Mom told me that one day, with "the paisa Ospina," she went to *Tierras Colombianas* where "El Patrón" Romero used to have lunch. When "the paisa Ospina" introduced her to the capo, Romero said, "The friends of my *parces* are my friends." She said that, when her "paisa" went to the bathroom, she respectfully asked "the narco" for a favor.

Mom never said what the request was. Later, she denied ever seeing, let alone talking, to a kingpin.

The homeless introduced her to Osvaldo Gómez: "The Queen of Queens," a transvestite with a rose, green, yellow, and blue beard, whose companions were a parrot perched on his shoulder and a dog painted a thousand colors. Mom commented that "The Queen" probably received a few *pesos* from the cartel bosses because she didn't work and yet wore new dresses and feathers every day. In Cali York, every day, the sellers of watches, chains, marijuana, the whores, and the faggots (with tits and asses full of silicone) were chased by the police and the immigration agents. Most of these "little angels," in addition to snorting *coca*, were undocumented.

Mom never realized the danger we were in. If we left that slaughterhouse unscathed, it was sheer luck. On March 11, 1992, Mom, Adrian, and I had what we think of as a close call with the work of the *Cali*

Pachanguero hitmen. At 7:00 in the evening, the three of us went to the *Meson de Asturias* to pick up a seafood paella Mom had ordered over the phone. Two hours later, Manuel de Dios Unanue, a Cuban journalist for El *Diario/La Prensa*, was shot twice in the head. Unanue was murdered for talking about things he shouldn't have, things that upset the capo Santacruz Londoño.

Because of Mom, Adrian and I lived through some seriously distressing moments. I was turning sixteen and my brother was ten when, one morning, Mom went to her routine doctor's appointment but didn't come back home the whole day. My brother and I felt abandoned. That night, they called from the hospital to let us know Mom was being held in the psychiatric ward. Adrian's father had been to see her; however, he did not say a word to us about Mom's status. On the third day, I went. I felt like I was dying of grief and horror; yet, when I saw that pale, haggard, disheveled, barefoot woman dressed in an old white coat, I ran away. When she returned home, she told us the doctors had made a mistake, that everything had been a big mistake. As a precaution, and because Adrian and I were afraid of her, we slept together in the same room, with the lock on. We didn't know what was going on with Mom. Mom was crazy. We were horrified to see her scream for no reason, break glasses and plates, stick her head in the freezer, get rid of clothes, and cry non-stop.

Luckily, Mom started her new profession as a teacher and soon joined a group of bohemians who called themselves poets. Relating to young students and writers-in-the-making managed to soothe her. Mom worked at a high school in Upper Manhattan where she started teaching math and ended up as a special education teacher. She made the change, the license swap, because she was fed up with these kids who did not give a fuck about her scolding them and refused to learn how to solve a simple algebraic equation. When Mom turned sixty, she decided—overnight—to retire because, according to her, the air had become thick and it was difficult for her to breathe.

I kind of forced Mom to come to Florida. Even though we didn't live together, I was glad to know I would have her nearby. I had to convince my husband as well. "You should be nicer to my mother; it costs you nothing to tell her you like the idea of her coming with us to Florida. You will see, if you are kind, she will stop seeing you as the enemy." Just to see me happy, even when his mother-in-law made his balls swell with anger, Jack agreed to my request. He reluctantly helped to find her an apartment in one of those beautiful condos that have swimming pools, a gym, a Jacuzzi, a sauna, and other amenities. He also made sure it was in the center of the city where she would find people, restaurants, cafes, and shops so that she would not miss the hustle and bustle to which she was accustomed in New York.

Of course, this was not what she wanted. In Florida, summer was endless, people were always passing through—they were tourists with whom no relationship could be established—there were no friends, no poetry readings, no presentations of writers . . . . The art scene was painfully missing, which brought about a total lack of emotions. According to her, "The air, which smelled of freedom in New York, is nowhere to be found here. In Florida, there is no life."

To please me, she lived in this "horrible" land for five years until she could no longer take it and one day said to me, "Please, daughter, take off my shackles, free me from this torture. It's not that I want to abandon you; it's that I'm slowly dying: this heat burns my cells and makes me older by the day. I don't know . . . there is something perverse in this place. . . . It might be in the air, in the water, those wetlands . . . an evil that's driving me crazy."

In New York, there was what she called magic, a sort of magnet that drew her in, something that did not happen with me, despite being born and raised there. "Mom, you're no longer a *spring chicken*. Why do you want to go back to New York? Have you forgotten winter? Have you forgotten the snow? That damn cold that crawls all over your body, that freezes your hair, teeth, and nails?" I tried to dissuade her, make her change her mind. She replied, her eyes looking past me as if staring into the past, "What's wrong with that? I went through forty winters without complaints. It is beautiful to see the snowfall that, flake by flake, covers the trees with its whiteness, the roofs, the vehicles, the entire streets. More beautiful still is to be able to hold in your hand the snow particles, like tiny crystals resembling six-pointed stars." Imagine romanticizing things as insufferable as the cold and snow! My brother used to say that Mom rationalized everything to get things out of her way or to try and fix them. I used to answer these useless explanations and cheap speeches with "Stop fucking around."

If she wanted to leave, I knew I had to let her go. Anyway, it was not the first time she decided to say *Bye*. Mom was one of those people who loved being surrounded by people and wished to spend their lifetime studying and learning. She kept finding courses and lectures she needed to update herself with, to keep abreast of what was happening in the world. Books were not enough; she had to have live information, and people to discuss with, and these activities were always her best excuse to leave the house. I, on the contrary, was a homebody: I barely had any friends and focused on what was practical, with no need to fill my head with unnecessary information. And it wasn't that I didn't like to read. I did. I read books about things that interested me: books about crimes, famous killers, criminal investigations, and horror stories. I did not inherit from her a physical resemblance, nor her "way of being."

I don't know if Mom resented that I took after my father—whom she detested. My father was a good and simple man—and that was unbearable to her. As she confessed, my father had been the first man in her life when she was about to turn thirty, and she did not forgive herself for having waited so long—just to end up with a characterless fool. Because of genetics, I *had* to inherit something from her: I liked to live comfortably without having to kill myself working for it. Responsibility was one thing, but to strive for perfection, even for efficiency, or to amass a fortune, that was something else. Her motto, like mine, was to do things right using as little effort as possible and leave for tomorrow what we do not want to do today. I have to thank her for making my brother and me see things exactly as they are, without adornments. What we didn't forgive her for, especially my brother, was that she let us do our own bidding. I think she cared about us, and a lot, but she didn't know or didn't care to learn the art of being a mother.

Whenever I said that I was not interested in being a doctor because my vocation was not to save the life of any worm or that I did not lean towards the legal profession because I did not see myself defending criminals, or that I did not want to spend decades studying engineering (like she had done) and then not even know how to hit a nail, Mom answered, "Your life is yours and you have the right to live it as you please and to do what makes you happy. You are intelligent, daring, and skillful, and I know you will get a job that takes you forward. Now you are a teenager and that sweet bird, as they call youth, only allows you to see the delights of age. Sooner or later, at any given moment, you will feel an unknown force pushing you into the real world, where you will be solely responsible for what you do . . . and you will be afraid. . . ." When she said these words, she closed her eyes, and it was as if she were speaking to herself, "You will not be able to avoid it, you will be afraid to surrender to the blows of life . . . and it is not that fear is bad or good, it just is. It inhibits your spirit; it represses you, turns you into a coward."

That day finally came. That moment when life admitted no postponements and, for better or worse, everything depended on me. I became a policewoman, an agent for the criminal investigations department. My job was not easy. For eight hours a day I had to deal with human scum: thieves, murderers, rapists, traffickers, and madmen. The rules required being physically protected (bulletproof vest and helmet) and mentally alert; it required quick action to avoid getting caught in a stabbing or a shoot-out. My work looked nothing like the cops-and-thieves game my brother and I had fun playing, using water guns. What happened in the real world was akin to playing Russian roulette or getting in a cage with hungry tigers—one had to be really lucky to come out alive. Over time, my duties were limited to investigating and obtaining evidence at crime scenes. I confess that, in the beginning, the bodies (many torn to pieces), the blood, and the stench, provoked horror and nausea in me. After a while, they became simple occupational hazards.

I remember one of my first activities as a rookie. My partner and I attended a call from the neighbors at an apartment building where a guy with a gun robbed and injured three people. According to the informants, the attacker had jumped out and probably tried to sneak through the trees and bushes surrounding the building. My partner immediately climbed the walls to check around the courtyard. I, Beretta 92 in hand, ran to the front door of the building thinking the individual might have chosen to leave from the front. Just as I'd imagined, the guy was calmly carrying a lump in his hands. I immediately knew it was him because of his shock to find me there. He dropped the lump and reached behind his back where he possibly kept the gun. It was only a matter of seconds: moved by my instinct of self-preservation, before he'd reached all the way to his back, I shot him in the leg to immobilize him. When my partner came back to the car, cursing from frustration because he thought the suspect had escaped, he found him handcuffed.

I remember one experience quite particularly just because it was disgusting. My partner and I heeded the call of a group of citizens in Rego Park, where mothers took their little ones to play and the elderly met to talk. A man in his early forties or so, stark naked, was chasing after the children and shouting obscenities. We stopped the guy, forced him to put on his pants, and forcibly got him in the back of the vehicle. "Motherfuckers, I'm going to shit on you!" the deranged man shouted—and we found out he was being literal about it. He defecated on the seat and threw his shit at the separating board between the front and rear seats—a sort of metallic grill. The shit flew through the hundreds of tiny holes and sprinkled all over us. After vomiting in disgust, we took him to the psychiatric hospital instead of the police station. The nurses and doctors cursed us out for bringing this human filth to them. The vehicle, like many others in similar condition, was auctioned off.

It is unfair how the media reports only what suits them or what is politically correct. The details of what actually happens are generally omitted. There is never mention of the hell that law enforcement agents go through or the shit they endure daily. This treacherous machine misleads people into accusing the police of brutality, taking to the streets to protest, raid shops, burn cars, and endanger the lives of others while glorifying criminals. "My color matters," "Supremacist terrorist," and "I am humanX," are some of the sensationalist slogans used to confuse and manipulate public opinion, and to placate and please certain minority groups. Mom, even while ignorant of all the conspiracies and all the dangerous and disgusting occurrences that were part of my job, one day, proudly, told me, "Perhaps at the cost of mistakes and risks, you are managing to embrace the strong, courageous, and wonderful woman you carry inside. Daughter, you are a warrior!"

Mom, you don't know, it's been years and I still remember those words. I feel like that warrior, that wonderful woman you see in me. I don't understand why it was so hard to tell each other how we felt. Maybe it was because you didn't know how to do it, because I'm a jerk, or because, ultimately, we are the same.

Before I go back to the hospital, I put lipstick and blush in my purse because I know you like to look good even in your worst moments. I remember that you asked for a little color on your cheeks and lips that time you were bedridden with the infection caused by the disgusting needle with which you had your ankle tattooed, or when you went to the hospital with that potassium drop that overwhelmed your whole body. "Mom, we are in time. I'm confident. Mom, we still have a lot to share—I know, I feel it," I say to myself while walking the hospital's hallway to your room. "Mom, I accept you as you are. I promise you that, as soon as I return to your side, I will tell you I am proud to be your daughter. I will tell you I love you as many times as necessary. Mom, I love you."

One of the most striking things about my sister is how tremendously self-confident she is. It is difficult, I would say "impossible," for anyone to impress her. For Elina, it is one thing to admire a person and another to feel overwhelmed, restless, or excited about them. Emphasizing her position, she repeats what for me is a shocking, vulgar phrase, nothing "Gucci": "From this *matraca* world of shit nobody escapes: the priest shits, the pope shits, and even the most beautiful woman leaves her pile of poop in the toilet."

My sister came to the United States when she was very young—without malice and as a complete idiot. Two decades later, when we met again, I found that she had become someone else. She no longer trusted anyone's stories or believed in foolishness like preserving good manners, smiling, and being kind to everyone. She had stopped giving sacred respect to others, the respect they thought they deserved even if they were bitches. My sister had learned the difficult art of saying things that seemed innocent but were said intentionally to hurt sensitivities or make gratuitous enemies. She didn't even believe in "Our Father" prayed on your knees. On the other hand, I have been living in New York for more than two decades and have yet to overcome the fascination the people of my country have for the famous, the rich, and the beautiful. It is difficult for me. It is not easy to leave behind this frivolity; I am easily dumbfounded by beautiful people, dazzled by important men and women—who are also beautiful. If I must describe a person, I put the word cute, beautiful, "Gucci" first . . . the rest is secondary and irrelevant. For me, if you're ugly, you're fucked—even if you're the nicest and kindest person out there.

My two husbands were handsome men. I married them because of their cute faces with no regard for the fact that they were shameless, women-exploiting players. The first one had green eyes that drove me crazy despite my knowing that he was sadistic and abusive. The very night of our marriage, he verbally assaulted me and treated me like a thing, an object that belonged to him. After cutting the wedding cake, he forced a chunk of it into my mouth. He wounded my palate with the spoon and laughed about it—pleased. I realized right then and there what was coming, but, stupidly, thought that my love would sweeten him, that I could change him. As if one could ever change a beast or a psychopath. I must have been crazy myself to endure him slapping me, punching my eyes black, and dragging me on the floor by my hair whenever he was mad or frustrated because things had not gone as planned. My house and my car became his property, and my savings and salary, far from insignificant, went to his private account. And I thought he loved me when his beautiful green eyes shed crocodile tears so that I would continue to loosen my money his way.

As a gift of appreciation for the good life I gave him, he gave me a purebred dog. All the scumbag wanted was to humiliate me. With sorrow and anger, I saw how, on the first bath, the "pedigree" animal's ears came off and the beautiful golden-brown color washed away. One day during a hurricane, the damn dog ran outside and he forced me to go out after it. The animal stepped on an electrical wire the rain and wind had knocked to the ground and instantly died—charred like some forgotten meat in the burning grill. Seeing the poor dog electrocuted gave me a fit of laughter. I went back in the house laughing my guts out and continued laughing out loud despite the repeated slaps the son of the bitch gave me. I laughed at seeing the stupor on his face, his fury, my luck at thinking that the electrocuted body out there could have been mine . . . . I laughed at my idiocy for having chosen a husband as miserable as that asshole.

That's when I arrived in New York: escaping from that damn man. I didn't learn my lesson though. I stumbled over the same stone again when I chose another handsome "bacanito" to be my second husband. This man believed himself to be a medieval gentleman: he wore a Sean Connery-style beard and stood impressively tall. I looked at him once and my mind got clouded, even though my instincts (that infamous sixth sense of women) tried to alert me to his potential danger. I don't know what chemical elements or hellish components shoot up through our nerves to warn us, but any such sign was in vain because I was spellbound. Before me, within my reach, I had that handsome "Gucci" I wanted to conquer when, clearly, it was he who had decided not to let a precious prey escape. I wanted to live life with him at any cost. I didn't care what came next: insults, abuse, theft . . . . If that was my destiny, I accepted it in its entirety.

When that fate was fulfilled, I could not complain—there I was trapped once more in the same situation. This man, like the other, resented my intellect, and could not stand my position as a doctor, to be respected and surrounded by feelings of love and friendship. It bothered him to feel that everything he lacked in the world had been given to me—he never stopped to consider my efforts and sacrifices to get everything I had. If I hadn't been convinced of my worth as a human being and as a professional, the emotional scourge this guy caused me would have torn me to pieces.

Everything came back: the humiliations, the criticisms, the insults, the words circling constantly around me until I felt guilty for deeds I had not committed. It was like living the same moments again as if life offered no other options. Damn! How hopeless! Years wasted next to that pair of selfish abusers and all for my frivolity, for looking only at physical beauty and not knowing how to appreciate the qualities that make a human being a good person. I laugh as if it were funny these things that really hurt me. My sister tried to hide the anger that my behavior produced in her, my carefree attitude and the silly and naïve way in which I excused these scoundrels' abuse. She didn't know that this was the only way I knew to get by and out of the pain.

Either way, I still do not fully understand this mysterious and perverse game that is life —where little can be done against the laws imposed by the human condition. Or is ours really a predestined fate? Because we know what's going to happen, yet, whether we like it or not, we can't stop things from happening. My sister says that a man and his destiny create each other. From the beginning, we realize that what we say or do will lead us to misfortune and yet we do not stop; rather, we open the door to doom. Fate looms and calls us. We could dodge it, turn our backs on it, and move away, but we don't. On the contrary, we invoke it, tempt it; we do not let it go and, without realizing it, we obey it. Only when one reviews the facts left behind does one become aware of their overwhelming force. It is then that man suffers and laments the fate he has forged by himself. Many times I have wondered if happiness is a part of destiny. My sister reminds me what Camus says about it: *The human heart has a tiresome tendency to label Fate only what crushes it. But also, happiness likewise, in its way, is without reason since it is inevitable.* In the end, I believe our humanity probably lies in that useless struggle against the inevitable. We are absolute masters of our days—destiny belongs to us.

Definitely, my sister and I are different. She is practical, nihilistic, daring, irreverent. Many times, I look at her when she is still and quiet. In her eyes, I discover a certain strange glow and wonder what terrible things go through her head. Behind her gaze hides (I do not know) something indefinite, passions that she keeps in her soul—which, with a certain resentment, make me think of the creatures hidden in the undergrowth. Our mother, Toby, told me that, when we were little, her stepfather was poisoned and stood on the brink of death. Of course, Toby was glad to see the old bastard kicking and convulsing—he surely deserved it. However, she had had nothing to do with the poisoning—although she always wished he would just drop dead. Toby suspected that my sister was to blame. That little girl was weird. She spent most of her days hiding under the bed and, at night, instead of sleeping as all normal children do, she would stand by the window and stare at the sky. People thought she was mute. She never said a word despite knowing how to speak and, the few times she did, it was to mention the huge-horned monster with goat feet. That girl was a devil in disguise: she screamed and kicked as if possessed whenever anyone of us (or outsiders) tried to touch her or, worse, caress her. She poured the poison into the oatmeal drink of that bastard everyone called Grandfather. She knew well where our father kept the 1080 for the rats. She also knew which cup the scumbag always used.

I can't deny my sister has her own wicked ways—which make her oddly special. She was proud to be the niece of Alejo, a delinquent who was our father's younger brother. In the village where Dad and his siblings were born, it was rumored that Alejo had escaped to the mountains after stabbing a guy to death—the man had stolen a pair of donkeys from him. My sister applauded the fact that the uncle had the guts to kill whoever had hurt him. Nonetheless, however weird she may be, trying to poison someone was too crazy, even for her. I do not believe she could do it—much less as a child.

To my sister, all human activity is normal. She says bad passionate affairs, those wastes of the human soul that embarrass us, are part of the nature of man. Therefore, we can condemn them, but should not be scandalized by them— because it is perfectly human to do evil. For me it was fine to curse, but it was not "Gucci" to discuss the thorny subject of sex and, whenever she brought it up, I was on guard. I think that, because I was a doctor, I had no problem with nudity. Every day I check the bodies of men and women showing their genitals. I show myself naked without shame, if I must, because the human body is for me only an instrument, a representation of the being that must be cared for and healed when sick. However, I don't feel comfortable talking about sex, about intimate things that I consider belong only to me.

She made fun of my views on sexuality, especially when I bragged about not feeling carnal urges—especially after leaving youth behind. Out of indoctrination rather than modesty, the women of my country are demure. My sister said that we all—especially the women of our generation—are but repressed hypocrites. We pretend to be shocked. We deny that we enjoy sexual relations. No one admits that they masturbate, that they use a dildo, a vibrator, when they feel *the urge*. All this is the result of the poor, manipulative, and castrating education we receive. We girls did not undergo the mutilation of our genitals as practiced in Africa and the Middle East, but our clitoris was cut off emotionally. To admire a man's physique (or, worse, to brush up against one of them) meant to be a whore. My sister tells me that she learned to enjoy the disgusting way a man looked at her, a behavior that she once considered indecent and made her feel dirty. It often happened to her before she reduced her breasts and threw away that "dairy cow disgrace."

She possessed huge tits and could not help but provoke in men the desire to at least enjoy them with their eyes. But from looking to touching there was a big difference. It wasn't until 2017 that women who had experienced sexual harassment were empowered, especially in their workplaces. The movement called "*Me Too*" gained momentum when famous Hollywood stars filed sexual abuse allegations against Harvey Weinstein, film producer and owner of Miramax. The movement resulted in the empathy of society giving women the courage to talk about their ugly experiences.

"I, like most women, was also abused," my sister confessed. "I was still the fool who came to the United States when the doctor who examined me, a son-of-a-bitch Cuban, massaged my breasts, rubbed himself against me, and introduced his disgusting cock between my legs. I didn't know what to do; out of shame I didn't tell anyone, not even my husband, and I've kept it a secret until now that women can talk, and we know we're victims. Our bodies or the clothes we wear are not a reason to be violated. We are not guilty of male immorality, or of their hormonal imbalance. I swear to you that, if that had happened to me a few years later, that scumbag would have had his eyes and testicles torn out before he was reported to the authorities to be buried in prison."

Moved by her courage, I told her about an embarrassing secret I'd kept for years. It had been three years since my arrival from Ecuador and one since my marriage to my second husband when, at one of the parties he organized to boast that he handled money (my money), one of his friends followed me to the bedroom, closed the door, grabbed me from behind, covered my mouth, and raped me. The bastard threatened to kill my months-old daughter if I dared to scream. Since I was an idiot, I believed him, and let that miserable prick get away with it. Sometime later, I told my husband, just to rub in his face the kind of vermin he brought to our house. I instantly regretted it because my humiliation didn't move him. It seems that he thought I was defaming his dear friend. My sister said that whenever there was consent, copulating, fooling around, fucking, or whatever the sexual act was called, was as normal as drinking water to quench thirst. If at any time she stopped having a partner, it was because age made her a demanding woman. She realized that she no longer had the desire to discover the nooks and crannies that men hid under their smiles and pretty words, nor did she have the time to deal with another guy. "Oh sister," she said, "things change. A relationship requires a tremendous amount of energy and, over time, the presence of the same man and routine tire. It is better to have a casual adventure, let a man surprise you, and then, well, goodbye. I confess that it still excites me to see a male roar just like a beast. However, the same pleasure can be achieved without having to mix one's own flows with the fluids of other bodies."

My sister denied being romantic; however, her eyes shone and her voice trembled when she talked about that man she met in adolescence, whom she visited every time she returned to Ecuador. She was excited to remember the way he moved his lips when he spoke, how he tilted his head to the right to look at her, his energy as he squeezed her in his arms. Any desire to wallow with a man was kept for him. That man was ideal for her because whatever short time they occasionally shared did not allow her to learn about his flaws. That was perfect love, the love that did not pale or die because separation and distance protected it from routine and disappointment.

I chose my husbands because they were handsome. My sister chose them because they were convenient. The first man helped her, in part, to pay for her university studies, and the second one helped her to start the textile business she owned. My sister believed that, as with any other human relationship, this coexistence was a two-way deal: giving and receiving from both ends. The first husband was an ugly guy I would never have looked at. The man was no "Gucci," but he promised to work, to offer her what she needed while she was pursuing a career. From the beginning, my sister knew that this relationship was not going anywhere because she did not feel any attraction or admiration, not even an iota of affection for him. She confessed to me that he was the kind of man whose personality, character, and cock she detested the most. And since what is not born cannot grow, she had no qualms about finding herself a lover and, as soon as she was able to, ending that farce that was her marriage.

"Sister, did it ever cross your mind that your husband would kill you if he discovered your betrayal?" A man, no matter how good at heart, cannot bear to have his pride hurt. In the soul of all human beings, wild passions are hidden, and there are times when those passions escape from their lairs eager to find prey, hurt it, kill it, and devour it. I tell my sister it is difficult for a man to tame these beasts, no matter how useless the cause, because passion does not understand the mandates of reason—especially if those unleashed are resentment and revenge.

Killing to get revenge, to get rid of a rival, to punish an unfaithful woman. Humans possess the ability to bend their thumbs to grasp things. This eventually taught man how to wield a knife, a weapon. With this ability, Brutus killed Caesar. King David took advantage of such skill to get Uriah, Bathsheba's husband, out of his way and seize her. My sister believes that a man like her ex-husband (not only a good man but also a fool) couldn't have the guts to kill even an ant. According to her words, this man had a huge cock and very little self-love. I believe, instead, this behavior is not a matter of self-love, but a lack of love in general. This man did not love my sister, so her betrayal was rather a liberation.

The lover my sister had while she was married to her first husband became her second husband. The guy wasn't handsome (he thought he was) nor was he ugly either. My sister confessed her intentions were to have a good time with that brute with *capo* airs, without getting involved and without commitments. I think she, perhaps influenced by the experiences lived in a culture different from ours or the little value she placed on virtue and moral qualities, had no awareness of fidelity. For her, only the desire to live, to live according to her rules, counted; more so if there was a fascination with danger. If I had done something like this, I would have felt not only sinful but worthy of the gallows and hell. I wonder how I could look straight at others again, enjoy the breeze, or watch the rain fall without feeling despicable. It was not my intention to condemn my sister for her ways—never thinking about consequences or the harm she caused her children. I just wanted to ask her questions. Ask her . . . well, what could I ask her?

Among so many things that I simultaneously admire and dislike about my sister, the arrogance and contempt with which she expresses herself about others, stand out. "I was already a 'shitty retard' for a long time and, at this point in life, I would not continue to be a fool and let myself be abused by an asshole. They can call me petty, stingy, but I'm not going to hand over what I've earned to any pimp wanna-be," that's what she said. And she lived by it.

My sister is a "bacanita," a hard nut to crack; she's not like me. If someone cries to me or tells me their sad stories, right then and there I loosen the bills. For years, I worked like a mule to be able to send money to my country, so that my family, especially my nephew, could enjoy life—not only a comfortable life but a luxurious one. My sister advised me not to suffer for others, to let everyone scratch with their own nails, or maybe I hadn't realized that I was being ripped off. "You're here suffering while they are over there living great lives," she told me so that I would stop feeling compelled to make others happy. I thought she had become selfish and irresponsible. Because of her practical ideas, she would not be obliged to do anything or be held accountable to anyone. When my sister left the country or was taken out of the house as she complained, we knew that she suffered abuse and humiliation, but at the same time she managed to disengage from all family ties. We were the others, the ones who were left behind, who had to comply with the family, and when the old folks got sick, it was our obligation to provide them with care, help feed them, and wash their butts. When our mother died, my sister arrived at the funeral. Forced by a sense of commitment, she approached the coffin, looked at the corpse sideways, and did not even pretend to shed a tear. Family and friends were pained by her callousness.

When I came to New York, I was already a practicing doctor in my country. I brought with me years of practice that would be of little use in a technical country where codes and protocols did not make way for experience, where a certificate, a permit, was the only guarantee of skill. I had to learn that this new world was a machine and that professional advancement required bending and hiding what was called "expression of feelings." The hugs and *te quieros* that were normal in the culture I came from had to be repressed if I wanted to be part of the medical gears of the mega society.

I remember the small town where I complied with the obligatory rural practice in my country. A miserable little town on the border with Peru, so poor that sudden death was a sort of lucky strike. The inn where we interns stayed had been converted into a housing project, and the road that took me to the medical center was pure dirt. The rains left puddles and mudflats that soon became a breeding ground for vermin. Looking at the cane stalks and rusty zinc roofs, as well as the chickens, dogs, goats, donkeys, and filthy children, I thought Guayaquil, my native city, was paradise—and I had lost it. It was not easy to understand how the poor could survive in that environment fate had dealt them. As a doctor, I compared poverty to a wound in the body, a wound with which one lived hoping it would heal one day and thus one could continue through life, between brief moments of joy and the enormity and sadness of reality. In those moments, I understood why the poor embraced Christ—that miserable man screaming in pain nailed to some pieces of wood—and took him as a traveling companion. Only in this way, believing in Christ, could they endure the present pain—in hopes of a better life beyond death.

The small construction of brick blocks where the health center operated had ten beds, of which half were occupied by women in labor and the rest by stabbed, battered women, and raped girls. One day, a dirty and bloodied girl arrived at the consultation with her mother. The patient appeared to be twelve or thirteen years old. Her skin was dark, dry, and cracked by the sun; her bones, barely covered by the dermis, demonstrated a high degree of malnutrition. According to their statements, the minor had been sexually abused by six border police *guardias*. As I healed the wounds caused by the brutal attack, I learned that the girl was seventeen years old, and, together with her mother, they took care of a herd of pigs that they shepherded around the town in search of leftover food (for themselves and the animals). Hours later, the girl had a fever, vomiting, and convulsions. She died at dawn.

These symptoms led me to the conclusion that something else had happened to her besides multiple rapes.

This was confirmed when I discovered the cause behind this girl's death. My task, in addition to treating the patients, was to document every procedure and result obtained in each case. As the small medical center did not have the necessary equipment and material to perform a forensic operation, I devised my own way to do it. With a hacksaw and a drill, I cut her head open. To my shock and utter disgust, hundreds of worms gushed out from her brains. Rape was a despicable event that coincided with a terminal case of trichinosis. This disease was caused by the tapeworm cyst—this parasite is acquired in larvae form through the consumption of infected pork meat.

The mother went to court and accused the rapists, "Those men killed my daughter," even though the girl had died from causes that had nothing to do with rape. Sadly, in that miserable little town, nothing could be investigated, much less proven, so that is where the story ended: the *guardias* never faced a trial either for murder or rape.

During my time in practice, I found situations typical of these villages where people's lives were worth the same as that of a stray dog stoned to death by strange kids or crushed by a passing vehicle. Being born and dying were but the same thing—incidents that happened every day. For many mothers, their pregnancies were as common an occurrence as being fat or having parasites—the possibility of a child, but an afterthought.

Many times, I heard conversations like this one among pregnant women:

"What's wrong with you, *Comadre*, with that huge belly?"

"I think I've eaten too much fried pork."

"No, *Comadre*, I know what's happening, I tell you because it has already happened to me three times: that belly is full of worms. No better remedy than tamarindo on an empty stomach to cure that."

At the time of giving birth, they realized they were bringing another hungry child into the world.

The government decided at some point to stop the growth of the poor's population. To achieve this, nurses and midwives, armed with chloroform, knocked out the most naïve and informed them of the dreaded package of worms that had been luckily removed from their stomachs. Others came out with stories of a slippery creature that, like a fish, slipped away and ended up in a bucket by the bed. I reported these atrocities to the authorities. What was happening was nothing "Gucci." They were killing newborns—indeed, as lightly as if killing worms. The administrator called the police. The officers wrote a report and then made the respective investigations. Sadly, midwives, administrators, policemen, and judges obeyed their superiors' orders and things did not change.

I did not know whether to believe her or not when Pascualita Quiñones, an old nurse, told me that my claims would be useless. In the 1960s, no one could prevent poor women from being sterilized with the medicines provided by a social plan called "Alliance for Progress." "Improving the lives of all the inhabitants of the continent" read the propaganda for this U.S. economic-political-social-aid program for Latin America, proposed during the administration of John F. Kennedy. According to Pascualita, preventing more poor people in Latin America from being born was a way to improve the lives of the American people. My report went to a drawer—and everything remained the same.

Later, when I got to the United States and was studying to meet the requirements and pass the necessary exams for the license to practice medicine in this country, I worked in a private clinic. I insisted that in this country things were perfect, forgetting that we dealt with human beings and, in the night of their souls nested the same passions as everywhere else: vanity, selfishness, envy, hatred, revenge . . . . The director and owner of the medical center, supposedly, was my friend. We had gone to medical school together in Ecuador. However, she did not think twice about forcing me to attend to her patients while, at the same time, work as an ultrasound technician, a nurse, and an assistant in minor surgeries. I was practically her slave, working twelve to fifteen hours a day, including weekends, and for the same regular salary. Only necessity and my shitty-sufferer character made me endure such abuse and humiliation. I didn't even think about complaining or denouncing her. On the contrary, obedient to my stupid way of thinking, I thanked her for the favor she did me.

I had been taught and continued to believe that friendship was the noblest feeling among human beings, and that altruism and willingness to help were indispensable. I understood that friendship was a service, and I had no right to demand loyalty or reward from anyone whom I'd accept as a friend. For her, friendship surely meant something else, and she did not hesitate to take advantage of my knowledge. My sister rightly accused me of Stockholm syndrome. I accepted it. It was in my character and nature to suffer humiliation without protest—instead, I tried to protect and defend those who caused me harm. I don't know how many times I told my sister to "stop putting her feet in my soup"—in other words, to fuck off. "If I gave away my time and my energies to my boss, if I wasted my money on my nephew, if I supported my husband, those were my problems. Do you envy those lucky enough to count on me?" This is how I responded, unconscious of my foolishness, believing I was a "bacanita."

I was twelve years old when my sister traveled to the United States. Back then, we thought she had been invited to spend three months at our aunt's. Months and years passed and she did not return. One painful day, I heard the elders comment that the trip had been an excuse to allow the poor fool to do something worthwhile with her life. That vacation trip was a plan to get rid of the hindrance that she was and it would allow the remaining four siblings left behind to enjoy a more comfortable life. Sometimes, facts are sad consequences of other facts. One does not sin by what one does, but by the intention with which one does it. In the end, that trip benefitted my sister—despite being an act of cowardice by our mother which I could never applaud. I ask for forgiveness and compassion for our mother. I know that Gilly, my sister's daughter, has tried futilely to do the same. Gilly has encouraged her to forget what her grandma did, to remember only the good things, because, thanks to her, she went to school and learned how to read and write. Our poor mother's sin was ignorance.

"She did not give you affection or attention, but she never let you go hungry," I tell my sister, interceding for the old woman, knowing that this fact is an open wound in her soul that will hardly close. I think a million years may pass, but my sister won't forget or forgive. With bitterness, she says, "Maybe that lady was a good person. She was a good person to you, maybe to the other children, too . . . but not to me. She gave birth to me because she found no way to abort me. She confessed this to me one day. She did not care—did not realize even, perhaps, how her words hurt my soul. She raised me just as she raised the dogs and cats we kids brought home, but she never offered love or tenderness—there is not a single thing I can remember fondly that came from her."

I insist and tell her that she is no longer young and will soon feel the ailments of age: bitterness, remorse, horrible nostalgia for what was left behind . . . and she will realize that life is responsible for collecting and settling accounts. "Possibly my children will come to feel resentment for what I did wrong. I will suffer. I will feel miserable about it, but, right now, only my feelings matter. I don't feel pity for her, only this disdain that in a way is a form of revenge." Even today, almost fifty years later, my sister resents that time—and all the mess that caused her so much regret. Pessimists say, "That was my destiny. I had to fulfill it. I was destined to go through it. You ought to realize that only what must happen happens. My house was my family and I was kicked out of it for being a fool, the useless one." Our mother thought of my sister as both crippled and dirty. This was the reason why she was never able to show any love for her. And the reason behind this rejection is a secret that hurts me to such an extent that I will not even remind myself of it. Nothing will ever come out of my mouth that could damage her or cause her more pain. I cannot and should not bring this secret to light.

My sister is tremendously intuitive though. She asked a couple of times as if fishing for answers she sensed I was hiding, "When I had sex for the first time I did not feel pain or see the blood other virgins always talked about. Did something happen to me? Something bad that I can't remember? As a child, maybe? Do you know?"

I gave her a medical explanation, and told her that some women have what's known as "elastic hymen" and penetration does not cause them rupture or pain. I do not know whether she believed me or not. She remained silent, her gaze lost, rummaging through some nook and cranny of memory for a hint. Suddenly she asked, "Do you know Schrödinger's cat paradox?" Since I didn't know it, she explained that it was an experiment: a cat and a jar with poison in it are placed and sealed inside a box. There is a 50% chance that the glass jar could break. If the jar breaks, it will let the poison escape and, consequently, it will kill the cat. The interpretation of quantum mechanics implies that, for anyone not looking inside the box, the cat is simultaneously alive and dead. If one opens the box and looks inside, one can see whether the animal is alive or dead, not both. The experiment shows that observation determines reality. I couldn't understand what that cat story had to do with her virginity until she said, "I'm not going to worry about something I'm not aware of. Your secret is not part of my memory; therefore, if you keep it, it is your reality. Whether you want to tell me or not is your choice. Just don't come to me with comforting hugs; you know I hate all that crap. You also know I am not a helpless soul who would hang herself or cut her veins. So, don't fuck with me!"

There are things expressed in words and others that do not need them. I say this because there's a painting that leaves my sister in awe-induced silence no matter how many times she sees it. The Metropolitan Museum is huge and has rooms and sections dedicated to all the different styles, movements, and eras in the history of art. However, every time my sister visits it, she goes to the same room—it seems like a magnet attracts her to the same place. The room is dedicated to the works of surrealism. There are paintings by Dalí, Miró, de Chirico, Magritte . . . . Among them, there is that particularly "Gucci" painting in which a teenage girl appears with her hands on her head, lost in her thoughts, and unaware of the world around her. The girl, sitting in a suggestive posture, lifts one leg and shows her panties. *Thérèse Dreaming*, by Balthus, has been accused of being an apology for pedophilia and censured for showing a morbid eroticism far from innocence—denying that it is the spectator, with their malice, who stains the girl's candor.

"Let's see the new exhibit and then go back to your favorite room," I tell my sister, trying to get her away from what I consider a danger. It is in vain, for in the depths of her soul lives the harmful desire to discover something that she senses, an odious reality, the arrival of a destructive light, a light that breaks the darkness like that of a possibly fatal ray. My sister approaches *Thérèse Dreaming* without looking at the other paintings in the room. She addresses it with the same stealthy movements of a hunter in the footsteps of a wild animal. She stops in front of the painting and the spell occurs: like *Thérèse*, oblivious, she ignores the world around her, is imprisoned in her thoughts and immobilized by her concerns or perhaps by her fears. I don't know to what worlds her mind travels. Mute, she breathes slowly, her face showing no expression at all. I tremble, thinking that in some corner of her memory there will appear a hint of that event that must remain forever in the past. For a moment, she turns her gaze and, when she looks at me, I think she knows something, that she imagines things, that the symbolic language of the painting has sent her a signal and offered her the answer I will never be able to give her. I do not want to add any more pain, one last blow that would complete the breaking of her life—it was but a single damn moment in that childhood that she has forgotten. I hug her, wanting to protect her, then I take her by the hand and gently lead her away, so she can explain to me, once again, the symbolism in *Ariadne*, that dark painting by De Chirico.

There are phrases and quotes that my sister repeats in her literary work: *Revenge is not a fact; it is a state of rejoicing, in which the soul reaches the purest and most powerful emotion. Lex talionis, the law of talion, the law of Hebrew blood, the law of Mesopotamian retaliation: an eye for an eye, a tooth for a tooth.* Or what Lamech said to his wives in Genesis 4:23-24: *I have killed a man for wounding me, and a young man for injuring me. If seven times Cain will be avenged, Lamech will indeed be seventy-seven times.* I have concluded that that is her motto. My sister says that killing another human being should be easy, but one must comply with social formulas and do away with the desire. "Remember when our mother raised the knife and in one fell swoop chopped off the chicken's head?" She asks me with glee. "Do you remember that, for Christmas, 'The Whore,' our mother's sister, killed the pig she'd raised in her yard? Both of their eyes were shining and smiling as the edge of the knife flashed and blood gushed from those animals' necks. You, I, and our siblings wanted to complain or scream in sorrow for the chicken and the pig; however, we did not do either, because the words had escaped our throats and, as if hypnotized, we looked at the atrocity with the same radiance in our eyes as they had. Those sacrifices taught me that killing is in our genes, in our blood, in our nerves . . . hidden deep in the human soul.

"You are a doctor," she says. "Your training and that Hippocratic oath you recite to convince yourself that your mission is to heal and save even the miserable, who have no reason to exist, have appeased the natural instincts of the species. However, your favorite books and TV series are those of crimes and serial killers. You glorify psychopaths like Ted Bundy and Jeffrey Dahmer, both physically good-looking (even murderers had to meet that requirement). Bundy, before being executed, confessed to kidnapping, raping, and murdering thirty women. And Dahmer, 'the Milwaukee Cannibal,' killed and dismembered the bodies of seventeen men and boys. This murderer and rapist ate parts of his victims' bodies that he kept in his freezer. When we watch episodes of your favorite series, you scream. Not out of terror, but out of a hidden excitement right before the homicidal scenes—the flame in your eyes betray that ancestral virtue that means to kill. You have noticed that Genesis, only to mention one of the sacred books in the Bible, records beheadings, sacrifices, and deaths . . . and they do not cause us horror or traumatize us because we believe that they are part of the divine justice of human inheritance.

"There is something pure and divine in the act of raising a weapon. Can you imagine Cain's ecstasy as he plunged that donkey's jaw into his brother's body? Abraham's pleasure at the moment of raising the knife to sacrifice Isaac? It doesn't matter that he did it to prove obedience to God; what counts is the father's perverse intention against his own son. With that same ecstasy and pleasure, the Baptist's head was also cut off. If it were not for the feeling of guilt implanted by the Christian faith in which we are educated and the juridical laws, surely many would already be in the other world with scrambled brains, and many others with their guts out and testicles sliced."

So says my sister, a frown of contempt on her lips. Triumphantly almost, she proclaims, "That's what literature is for: *fiction*, to punish without an iota of remorse those who screw with our lives. Since I cannot kill physically, I do it with a weapon as powerful and deadly as words are, and despite not professing any faith, as someone said, I repeat: killing and seeing a miserable man die make me believe in God."

These unconventional ideas (articulated in front of a doctor who knew little about literature, ignorant of that "weapon of words" and other unusual concepts) forced my sister to go find her light in a cell of a psychiatric ward.

When she told me about it, I was not surprised. Something like that was expected to happen at any time and to anyone who would talk about such things that no one in their right mind should ever say. She also told all her friends about her stay at the nut house—even though her husband advised her not to talk about an experience so embarrassing and warned it could bring her problems. This embarrassing experience gave her a certain halo of mystery and fascination among her fellow writers—or, rather, aspiring writers. Those crackpots she met weekly to share their "masterpieces" extolled her. For them, she was a heroine. She now possessed the necessary requirement to exercise the trade. Instead of being considered a stigma, a shame, madness was a divine grace, a symbol of the guild's own creativity that everyone would like to have. Her companions romanticized the despair and suffering of Edgar Allan Poe, the hallucinations of Tolstoy, the chaotic life of Virginia Woolf (who, of her own free will, filled her pockets with rocks and walked into the River Ouse to drown), the psychotic episodes and the desperate behavior caused by Hemingway's narcissistic and suicidal personality disorder.

That day, my sister says, she arrived at Elmhurst Hospital in Queens for her semi-annual check-up. The regular exams gave normal results, but since she complained to be a little sad, the doctor suggested that she join groups of people with common interests who could help her socialize, relax, and abandon the routine. "Let me tell you what happened," said my sister. "That was enough to let my tongue loose and get me in very serious trouble . . .

"I stared at the doctor's face and smiled:

'I've been attending a Gnostic group for several months now,' I replied naively. 'There, we study ancient doctrines and esoteric practices that bring us closer to knowledge of the self. We meditate and practice astral exits. Do not think that I am talking about self-suggestion, but about unfolding the power to separate the astral body from the physical.'

'Have you managed to do it?' the doctor asked ironically.

'Of course,' I said— still not suspecting the problems my words would bring me. 'I lie in bed and relax in such a way that no muscle puts pressure on the astral body and, mentally, I pronounce a mantra: *Om Soham,* I am He—for me, He is the universe—until I reach a state of drowsiness. I get out of bed and walk around the room feeling like I'm floating; my feet don't touch the ground.'

'So, you can walk on air?' The doctor asked sarcastically once again, and I continued.

'You can have dominion over the astral body just as you have over the physical body. That is why Carl Jung took psychoanalysis to a plane that transcends the functions of the human body; that is, the unconscious, a secret part of our mind that controls who we are.'

'Do you believe in God?' he asked, intrigued now.

'Religion is a way of understanding the world. I define myself as a pantheist, like Spinoza and Einstein; that is, we believe that the universe, Nature, and God are the same. God is not a particular entity or simple energy—the divine is present in the totality of things.'

'I see, you believe the same as Einstein, so you must know why the scientist said, *God does not play dice with the universe.*'

'Let's break that down: first, in that quote, God is a metaphor for the cosmos, and second, Einstein, convinced that the universe is mostly predictable and measurable, did not accept the lack of certainty established by quantum mechanics when it says that, behind all things, there is a world of tiny particles that are governed by chance.'

"To all this, the doctor rocked his head with suspicion and, without fully understanding these explanations, asked what I did for a living. 'I'm a writer,' I replied. 'I just finished a story in which this woman caresses with delight the knife with which she plans to kill her lover. She will do so during their climax; when a man is at his weakest and closes his eyes. Killing him will be a tribute to pleasure, an act of faith.'

'So, you're a writer—where can I buy your books?' the doctor, frowning, inquired.

'This will be my first. It is not yet published.'

'Do you have children?'

'I have two, a seventeen-year-old girl and an eleven-year-old boy.'

'Aren't you afraid to play with knives in front of them?' He asked, leaving me totally ignorant of where that meaningless question was leading. He raised his headset and asked for assistance. 'You know, you have severe psychiatric problems,' he finally said as two guys dressed in white came in, held my arms, and asked me to accompany them.

'What's going on? Where are they taking me?' I screamed as the two guys put me in a private elevator."

My sister tells me this episode sounds like the plot of one of her stories, but it really happened. And it was perhaps the most horrible and humiliating event of her life. To find herself, by force, deprived of liberty, without shoes, dispossessed of her earrings, her bracelets, wearing only a white robe, and placed in a cage as if she were a beast . . . this is something she would not want for her worst enemy.

"That first night, I spat out the pill they gave me to rest, and, of course, I could not keep my eyes shut because of the anguish, anger, and impotence I felt," she confessed indignantly at those outrageous events. "The next morning, two male nurses took me to the communal bathroom where two other patients were already completely naked. There, one of the nurses had me remove my robe and, with a hose, sprayed me with freezing water. According to them, cold water was a part of the therapy that would help me relax, and calm my nerves. Back at the cell, trembling like a plucked pigeon, I was handed rice, wheat porridge, and a peeled banana for breakfast. All the food of the day came with a plastic spoon for fear of leaving us in possession of an object with which we could hurt ourselves or attack the guards. I want to clarify that those beasts that watched us were not nurses, they were gorillas disguised in white coats. Several times during the day—nonchalantly, through the bars—the gorillas slid drawings of souls coming out of the body and a book whose cover showed angels with their wings spread wide. I looked at them sideways, pretending not to pay attention because I knew it was a trap. They were testing me. Since they thought I was crazy, they were encouraging me to scream or go into crisis. They succeeded with the young woman in the cell next to mine. They tied her up in a straitjacket, took her away, and I never saw her again.

"The next day, at two o'clock in the afternoon, the gorillas on duty took me to a room where a woman and two men were waiting for me. These three, more than health professionals, looked like members of the Inquisition. They looked at me the way one looks at a cornered rat. They mocked my knowledge and interests, made fun of my 'supposed' job as a writer, and then asked me idiotic questions—for which they demanded answers since they needed to measure the degree of my ailment. I had been classified as schizophrenic—on the spot, on my very first appointment.

'Do you know your name?'

'My name is Elina.'

'So, your name is not Spinoza? Or Einstein either?'

'Spinoza was a Dutch Sephardic thinker and Einstein a scientist famous for explaining the theory of relativity.'

'Last night we saw through the cameras how you were spinning in bed; we saw that you got up and walked in circles around your room, unable to rest.'

'Could you sleep on a stone mattress, with all the lights on, and the tremendous noise these gorillas make with their jokes and laughter?' I answered the inquisitors with another question.

'What day is today?'

'Wednesday the 22nd.'
'Can you levitate?'

'The mind is powerful.'

'Do you think you are an angel and can float in the air?'

'The power of the mind is infinite.'

'Can you fly?'

'Is it that you don't get tired of asking the same question, or are you mentally retarded?' I asked the woman who insisted on the flying question.

'Can you fly?' She went on, not giving an inch.

'If your mind is fragile, you will not be able to take off even from that chair,' I answered.

'Who is the current president?' The third doctor asked.

'Bill Clinton.'

'Do you like knives?'

'Doctors, do you like scalpels?'

'Respond and don't comment: do you like them or not?'

'If I were a cook or a knife thrower, I would probably like them, but I am a writer; I prefer words.'

'Do you hear voices?'

'I'm not deaf.'

'Do you see ghosts?'

'I thought ghosts were invisible.'

"They returned me to the cell and, when they locked the door, I knew what a life-sentenced person must feel and why the animals in cages in the zoo howled and roared. The rest of the afternoon I spent restless, desperate, willing to grab them by the neck, those unhappy incompetents who, because they had a degree, dared to run other people's lives. That night, I agreed to take the sleeping pill I was offered, so that I could escape from that hell where my words and my candor were thrown back at me like daggers. The next day was just as bad. The same hose bath, the ridiculous questions (especially by that damn woman), more books of souls floating out of their bodies. I was about to scream and they would have taken me away—tied up in a straitjacket the way they did with the girl in the next cage— if my son's father had not come to visit and convinced me not to do stupid things that would surely extend my stay in the psychiatric ward. The third day was the same. I thought, *one more day, and I will go crazy.*

"In the afternoon, during the interrogation, a new inquisitor was present. The miserable woman made him aware of the situation and introduced me as schizophrenic, manipulative, delusional, prone to violence, and of monotonous speech. Before starting with the same stupid questionnaire, the new doctor, who seemed to be the director of the unit, indicated that if I had minor children, the hospital would have to contact social services because my presence would be dangerous to the welfare of the minors. I trembled at the mere thought of losing my children to something as bizarre as a lack of appreciation for an individual. So, in addition to responding accurately, I also did so energetically and logically. The woman asked the questions again . . .

'What is your name?'

'Elina with an I.'

'Can you fly, hold on to the air?'

'We know that so far only birds and airplanes can do that.'

'Do you hear voices?'

'I am not deaf; I can perfectly hear what you are saying now.'

"The new doctor said it was enough: 'This lady is not only sane, but she is also ingenious and coherent. A family member can come and pick her up this afternoon,' he said, signing the papers that rendered my case concluded. Free at last from that nightmare, I gave them my daughter's name and number. From the cage, full of joy, I waited for the door of the unit to open and to see Gilly's face.

"My daughter, accompanied by a nurse, came in, looked at me, and immediately went back out. I couldn't believe what was happening when she did not return, and I spent the whole night crying—unable to fall asleep. I left at nine in the morning the next day when my husband came for me. It was only much later that my daughter confessed that seeing me inside that cage—pale, with scrambled hair and anguished eyes—she got scared and ran away. Several months passed before my children stopped being afraid of me and stopped sleeping together with the door locked from the inside."

My sister asked for my help to see if, I, as a doctor, could ask for her medical records in the hospital and delete the pages where she was labeled schizophrenic. She had already tried it during an appointment with another department: she took the bulky file and, tucking it under her arm, went to the restroom. She was unsuccessful though because one of the office workers had seen her and asked for it back. That autumn, my sister had started as a teacher. She knew she would be laid off if it were discovered that she had been diagnosed, erroneously or not, as somehow mentally alienated. Luckily, the hospital decided to begin digitizing all new data that year and sent the old files to be stored in the basement.

Today, my niece Gilly told me my sister had been hospitalized. The diagnosis was not yet known. *Hopefully*, I thought, *it is not one of her acts.* Anyway, I wished it was nothing serious and she could get out of the whole issue soon. She's not going to die, I said to myself. People like her, I don't know, love life, but act like they don't care, like it's all the same whether they're here or beyond the grave—and, for me, that's disrespectful. Life can't stand being taken lightly. But that's my sister, not "Gucci" at all. She drives me crazy. There are moments when I can't stand her. She tends to make random, off-hand comments (with no ill intention, she says) that hurt . . . and destroy. She knows very well how to use the right words at the right time.

I know her quite well, so I am not fooled by her arrogance disguised as modesty or the disdainful smile that she cannot hide. Her personality is detestable; her nihilism, unnerving. However, despite everything, I love her. I respect her. My sister is an amazing woman.

We met at the end of the last century, in 1995, when the Chilean J. Skármeta put a note in the Hispanic newspaper inviting people interested in literature to form a group. New poets and storytellers, purveyors of illusions and inflated egos, met on a Saturday in the South Bronx, in "The Bonfire," one of the classrooms of Hostos Community College in New York, from where very few of us managed to escape alive. In the ranks of the warriors willing to pass the trial by fire, as Skármeta called it— with a couple of bottles of *Casillero del Diablo* in his hands—were the candidates destined to write magnificent works and achieve glory. Among many other dreamers, there we stood, willing to risk our lives, if necessary, to see our words embodied in a book. We held our names high: J. Skármeta, E. Cano, D. Cortazar, J. Balzac, H. Sabato,

O. Rulfito, A. Vallejo, F. Ureña, J. Arenas, W. Paz, and me: R. Pacheco.

The reading of poems, short stories, fragments of novels, and then the judgments and suggestions on the texts presented, led us to great discussions and disputes. Balzac, "Mr. No Concessions," was relentless and slightly sour: he would disapprove of all work and ask us to throw it in the trash can. However, before reading any of his writings, in order not to be prosecuted himself, he announced that he did not grant permission to be criticized. Of course, it was useless for him to grant it or not (nor did it do him any good, either, to quote the real Balzac: *The more one judges himself, the less love he feels*, because, anyway, his *"magnum opus"* would be hurled into the many fires of judgment.) To iron out rough edges, there was *The Library*—the bar on the corner where we went to put an end to all types of controversy among Coronas, Heinekens, Budweisers, insults, and laughter—and, occasionally, a punch or two, accompanied by its respective black eye.

Many, offended by the harsh, brutal, sometimes fair, sometimes poisonous, criticism of their "masterpieces," were discharged, while other candidates were added to the potential springboard to fame and landed a position in the ranks of "the firing squad."

These were years of doubts, fears, and challenges. They were also years of madness and fun. For some, the workshop served as training. Through readings and commentaries on the work of the masters, destructive criticism, perverse judgments, and ill intentions, "the chosen" acquired the necessary tools for the craft. For others— the majority—it was just a place to socialize, to jump around the ring without daring to put on the gloves and give a quality fight. The thing was more complicated than arriving on Saturdays with a few bombastic lines (especially the self-proclaimed poets) that allowed them to inflate their egos and feel like Tarzan—and, like the man of the jungle, squeal like a crazy bird and beat their chest to show the chimpanzee Cheetah that they too were able to traverse the jungle jumping from one vine to the next.

"Compadres, you must read Vicente Huidobro, Pablo Neruda, Nicanor Parra," Skármeta recommended, his Chilean compatriots. "Those poets knew indeed that words are the mirror of thought, the order of the mind, and of the spirit." Excited, Skármeta continued with the rant, "In the beginning, God said, *Let there be light, and there was light,* and the word was the engine of creation, the word contained the unborn universe. Huidobro, a connoisseur of the word, created a movement whose goal was to make poetry an instrument of beauty and absolute creation. Let me recite one of his verses to you so that you can see that I am right:

> *Let poetry be like a key that opens a*
> *thousand doors*
> *A leaf falls; something flies by*
> *Let everything the eyes see be created,*
> *And the soul of the listener is trembling.*
> *Invent new worlds and take your word for it;*
> *The adjective, when it does not give life, kills.*

. . .

Why do you sing of the rose, O Poets!
Make it bloom in the poem.
Only for you live all things under the Sun.
The poet is a little God.

"Can you see it? With his words, he evaluates our ability to imagine, to move; he gives us the world, he leaves the gate open and the freedom to explore beyond the horizon." Old Skármeta recited the poem with his eyes closed and no one dared to make a comment. We let him continue without interruption. "My great friend, my *junta,* Pablo (Neruda), used language to talk about oppression, injustice, and the people's exploitation by the government, but also to provoke disgust, anger, and to call readers to action." Skármeta opened his eyes as his words flowed, "My friend, poet Neruda, believed in the illusion of utopia, of a better and egalitarian world, and was infected by the madness of the communists. He communed with Marxist teachings and the possibility of putting the working class in power, establishing social ownership of the means of production, eliminating social classes, and extinguishing the state as a form of domination of one class over the other."

It was Cortazar who interrupted Skármeta to express his surprise at these statements and wonder if Neruda was ever aware of this reality: "Seeing that the comrades stopped shouting slogans, abandoned the rifles, explosives, and fire that ignited the words, at some point Pablo had to realize that they never wanted to throw themselves into a bonfire and burn."

Arenas, the Cuban dissident, took the floor: "The militant comrades who defended the working class were not crazy. They never were. What they did have was faith that the revolution would catapult them towards a work of political importance, privileges, and royalties. A famous former guerilla fighter said, 'You have the right to take the best from life. You must take advantage of what you worked so hard to create. You're not always going to wallow in the mud, run with the peasants with a *petate* and a rifle on your shoulder, or eat rice as if you were Chinese. If I now wear the green uniform, boots, and beard, it is because it is in my interest to remain the glorious figure of the revolution. May starving morons continue to believe that the struggle for fucking ideals is going to pull them out of the sewer while I bring the water to my mill and fatten my cows.'"

While Arenas unmasked the defenders of the working class, the so-called Marxist comrades in the group seemed to swallow poison and looked at him with hatred. Ureña, eager to grab him by the neck, said, "You don't know true militants. They are faithful to ideas despite the facts, including hunger, misfortune, and the death of thousands."

Without considering the comments of Arenas or the furious "reds," Skármeta continued with his rant, "The non-poetry of the monkey men, of the self-proclaimed poets whose names I prefer not to name, consists of a string of extravagant and elaborate words that anyone can realize are taken from the dictionary. Words that no one understands, that they themselves do not know, abound in their verses. To make themselves look educated, each of the stanzas of these false poets is a jumble of Greco-Roman mythology, confusing the quarrels and exploits of Zeus, Aphrodite, and Hermes with Jupiter, Juno, and Diana. But Nicanor Parra, his anti-poetry and artifacts are something else! Listen to the following and tell me if I am wrong:

> *To lovers of beautiful letters*
> *I send my best wishes*
> *I will change the name of some things.*
> *My position is this:*
> *The poet does not keep his word*
> *If he does not change the names of things*
> *For what reason must the sun continue to be*
> *called the sun?*
> *I ask that it be called Micifuz*
> *The one with the boots of forty leagues!*
> *Do my shoes look like coffins?*
> *Know that from today on*
> *The shoes are called coffins*

Communicate, write down and publish
That the shoes have changed their name:
From today on they are called coffins."

I, taking an opposite angle, defended the poetry of Dario. I called him a "genius of modernism," the "father of avant-garde poetry," and, from memory, I recited a few of his verses:

The poet puts in his verses
all the pearls of the sea,
all the gold of the mines,
all the oriental ivory;
the diamonds of Golconda,
the treasures of Baghdad,
the jewels and medals
of the chests of a Nabad.
But since he did not have
to make verses or a loaf of bread,
when he finished writing them
he died of necessity.

Skármeta went into a rage and called me a filthy Mexican bohemian, *güevón*, son of a bitch. "How dare you mention him when we are talking about Nicanor!" For Skármeta, there was no one comparable to the poet Neruda, the anti-poet Parra, and his sister, Violeta. For Skármeta, "Gracias a *la Vida*," the song composed and sung by Violeta and popularized by Argentine folklorist Mercedes Sosa, was a sacred anthem:

> *Thanks be to life that has given me so*
> *much*
> *It has given me laughter and it has given*
> *me tears*
> *So that I can distinguish joy from*
> *brokenness*
> *The two materials that make up my song*
> *And your song, which is the same song*
> *And the song of all of us, which is my*
> *proper song*
> *Thanks be to life that has given me so*
> *much.*

Skármeta felt touched and said that he shared the same ballroom with Violeta during the First Outdoor Art Exhibition in Santiago. At the fair, he exhibited his first paintings and she showed her oils and embroidery on burlap. Then, he found her again in La Reina, municipality of Santiago, where he helped her assemble the poles of her tent like the canvas of a circus while stories were told— and then they laughed, sang, and recited Neruda's poetry. A little after composing the song, in 1967, Violeta took her own life with a pistol shot.

Decades passed, we got old, and, to this day, Skármeta continues to tell us about his encounter with Violeta. He continues to recount the Chilean legends about *The Trauco*, the seducer of women, and *the Pincoya*, the beautiful female who took men to the ship of death.

"Shhh! There is nothing special about those stories, they are the same as tales of *Tintin* and *The Pelada* in Ecuador. These characters are used to justify the promiscuity of hot women and make us believe in babies begotten by holy doves," Elina said the first time she heard the legends, ruining thus the sublime wonder of Skármeta's tales.

The anger begotten by Elina's teasing led Skármeta to call her "Cabrita," which in Chilean was translated as "Little Goat." Then, still not recovering from the bitterness, rehearsing a smile, he said, "I call you 'Cabrita,' so as not to call you 'Cabrona' (Scumbag)."

Elina did not hold back. "You're the cabrón!" she yelled. "You are used to the flattery from your bootlickers; you cannot bear to listen to what others have to say. Haven't you realized that we are not dogs that you can make jump and wag our tails whenever you want? You can call me 'Cabrita' or 'Cabrona,' but that is not going to break me, nor is it going to plug my soul. We leave that to the rotten and the spiteful, with all the crap they accumulate.

"*Rubén Darío* already said it," Elina added, emphasizing when pronouncing the name of the poet: '*You will have your own life to poison you.*'"

"Enough!" Sabato intervened. "Here one can no longer talk without initiating some scuffle. You, Skármeta, have the idea that we should all pamper you because you are the oldest and the leader. You, Elina, love to get away with your own ways and fuck with us. There must be a middle ground. To make that happen, we need to implement a law of respect and proceed in accordance with that law. Let's use the rules of traffic. Red light, *Stop*, forbidden to continue, give way. We are intelligent people. We can control our impulses and try to let go of selfishness."

Elina and Skármeta ignored the recommendations. They continued with their verbal war. Elina believed herself Tarzan's mother and sang the lyrics to a tango: *Life was and will be crap, in the year five hundred and ten and in the year two thousand . . .* while Skármeta thought that, because he was the leader of the group, he could do and say anything he wanted. The old man had us fed up with his thousand and one adventures of the eternal character Santiago, the painter. Skármeta was also an artist. It did not matter that Skármeta shouted and insisted that Santiago was not him because, equally for all the members of the group, these stories were the retelling of his experiences of youth. Santiago was Skármeta. Skármeta was Santiago. It was useless for him to be the oldest in the group, a man of experience, or to feign a serene, conciliatory posture—the knives of criticism also fell on his works and, like everyone else's, they went through the fire.

The truth was that no one escaped criticism: the sharp, cursed, and poisonous tongues of the good people who were the executioners of "The Bonfire."

Cortazar was the only judicious one in the group. His youth did not prevent him from looking around and discovering that life was a high-risk trade, that man was a problematic animal that could not stand himself—let alone others. In the constant discussions brought about by the "reds" in the group, he realized that the world was a dangerous place, with its resources poorly distributed, and that no revolution, neither the Chinese nor the Russian, let alone the Cuban, would change the status quo, the way Ureña, Vallejo, and other deluded people believed.

Arenas, a Cuban from Pinar del Rio, was often about to have a heart attack whenever he heard all the garbage coming out of the so-called communists' mouths. Trembling with indignation, he said, "Poor guerrillas trapped in the spider web woven by those damn birds of prey that were comrades Lenin, Che Guevara, Ho Chi Minh, and Mao." He found himself close to giving them a slap since he could not give them a bullet— he wanted them to scorch in hell. Instead, he entrusted them to *Blessed Santa Barbara, Babalú Ayé,* and *the Orishas,* to clear those minds brainwashed with a Molotov cocktail and to dry those tongues that spoke of wars and popular guerrillas without ever having seen a rifle in real life, or shitted in their underwear and wiped their butts with the leaves of the treacherous *jagüey*.

"How is it possible that these miserable folks dare to applaud revolutions that sowed misfortune and death in other people's countries?" he asked, deeply upset. "You do not know how privileged you are. While people in those countries ruled by communist rats suffered hunger, torture, persecution, and shrapnel, you choked on pizza with extra cheese, double-decker McDonalds with bacon, lettuce, and tomatoes, all properly accompanied by a liter of Coca-Cola. *No, chicos!* You pester the government that hosts you; you call it a shitty country while stupidly wasting your energy. You do not know what to do with the well-being and opportunities it gives you."

One day, twenty years later, when the group had disbanded and, from time to time, three or four friends would meet in Skármeta's studio on Canal Street, someone asked about Arenas' life. We had already forgotten when we had last seen him. Vallejo refreshed our minds with one of his half-intertwined tales: *We went to have a coffee and talked about literature and other things until, well, the Cuban could not swallow his own saliva since Fidel was in New York speaking at the United Nations, and he went, 'No, chico, how can it be so brazen, that scumbag, because I have him pierced here in my throat.' And then I followed with a rant of my own: that it is not that bad, after all, and things will likely improve between the two countries, and, you see, Castro does not seem like such a bad person and, surely, he should not carry all the blame. And that was the last thing I said to Arenas. He stood up, took his things, went out, and we never saw him again.*

That was in the late nineties when Castro visited New York. Elina said, "I saw Arenas later, at the *Gays' Parade* in the Village. He was walking hand in hand with his partner."

"I didn't know the Cuban was a faggot," Ureña said.

"How can you not know?" evil Skármeta asked, fixing his gaze on the two group mates. "Didn't you see how he crossed his legs, how he squeezed his buttocks when walking, and how drool dripped from his mouth looking at the crotches of Balzac and Cortázar?"

"Thanks to the fact that I am ugly, poor, and prone to marijuana, no one comes on to me, not even the *gay*," I said, gesturing as if I were holding a little roll of weed between my fingers.

"Now I understand his interest in inviting me to have a drink in his apartment," said Cortázar. "Now I understand the reason for his impertinent and out-of-place questions: he wanted to know if my girlfriend and I had oral sex, or if I liked to give it to her in the ass. 'That's my favorite practice,' he confessed to me, but I went on, like a big ball of words, without realizing that the Cuban was trying to give it to me."

Balzac, "Mr. No Concessions," kept quiet, putting into practice the wisdom of the Latino saying, "Flies don't fly into a closed mouth," although we all looked at him expecting a comment. We would have liked to know his opinion, even more so after that tender, melancholy story, full of humanity, which he had read to us a week before, where one summer afternoon the young character of the story had a strange encounter with another boy he never saw again. That would have been it, but Ureña continued to turn the matter around.

"These *'birds'* are not afraid to be infected with AIDS and die horribly like Rock Hudson."

"What a shame!" commented the malicious Skármeta, revealing his lack of scruples and dirty pedantry. "So handsome and macho he looked on the screen next to Doris Day and Gina Lollobrigida and, in real life, he was a butterfly. I do not know what is happening in this world; in my time, life was not so rotten. Today, they are all faggots. I, at this very age, still get horny. I have my girls with plump and hard meat who, for a thousand pesos, suck me and make me snort like a bull."

Elina looked at him with displeasure, her eyes stopped at his crotch, perhaps imagining a wrinkled and scrawny cock. Despite the experience gained in all his years of life on the planet, Skármeta had not learned to recognize that sexuality was neither good nor bad, it was not a matter of pigeonholing or defining; it was simply an innate aptitude, the most powerful and natural passion, a skill that was born with the human being. Old Skármeta was not able to accept that neither he anyone else owned the truth, nor did he know how to respect the right of each one to express their individuality freely. One of the bootlickers, whose name does not deserve to be remembered, a male mammal with a rhinoceros body and an underdeveloped brain, who, like many, had escaped the law of natural selection and managed to survive, jumped in with: *Leviticus 18:22 – You will not throw yourself with a man as with a woman; it is an abomination. Romans 1:27 – and likewise also men, leaving the natural use of women, ignited in their lasciviousness toward one another, committing shameful acts men with men, and receiving in themselves the retribution due to their loss. Corinthians 6:9...* "Stop the car!" demanded an angry Cortazar.

Elina could not help laughing—she found that morality and hypocrisy were one and the same. She said, "Based on what this *Homo Biblicum* has told us, we can come to two clear conclusions: one, same-sex attraction has existed since human beings inhabited this world. The thirst for carnal pleasure, that truth that resides within each one, in the cells, only recognizes and is relieved in another flesh, another flesh devoid of gender, race, origin, even species—passions typical of human nature that time has not been able to bend or tame." Vehemently, Elina continued, "Two: that the sacred books only condemn the male. We women are free to fully express our sexuality. Bad luck that these judges of antiquity applied banal and useless laws without wanting to recognize that females and males belong to the same species and that in our hearts, mind, and flesh, nest the same cravings for pleasure."

Ignoring Elina's words, Sabato and Ureña asked when she had last seen Arenas. "It was a few years after 9/11. I remember it because Arenas and I talked about the first group of prisoners to arrive at Guantanamo Bay, the detention camp that Bush Jr. established as part of his 'war on terror' program. Arenas, snorting like a beast, had cursed Bush, called him a despicable butcher who enjoyed the annihilation of those he considered enemies. 'Chica, you will see!' he had said. 'Those prisoners will be skinned alive, their souls will be torn off; he won't rest until they stop being human.'"

Elina told us the Guantanamo story told by Arenas. "In 2006, President Bush ordered fourteen 'highly dangerous' detainees to be transferred to the military camp at Guantanamo after being held by the

CIA in prisons outside the country. According to journalists and human rights groups, in those prisons, known as 'black sites,' detainees were interrogated under torture to confess to being terrorists. This group included Khalid Sheikh Mohammed, a mechanical engineering graduate of North Carolina Agricultural & Technical State University in 1986, who was believed to be Al-Qaeda's #3 leader before he was captured in Pakistan; Ramzi bin al-Shibh, alleged kidnapper during the 9/11 attacks, and Abu Zubaydah, suspected of being the link between Osama bin Laden and several Al-Qaeda cells. None of the fourteen 'dangerous detainees' were charged with any war crimes, yet on February 11, 2008, the Military System Commission charged them with committing the 9/11 terrorist attacks. That same year, the U.S. Supreme Court ruled that the Military Commission Act was not constitutional. However, the detainees remained in the military camp without charges."

Elina told us how Arenas could barely control his rage while talking about the political situation in his country. Arenas said he despised both the leaders of Cuba and those of the country that served as his refuge. "All these cursed ones were the same: they were moved by the same greed, the same selfishness; they thought only of themselves, of perpetuating the criminal order to protect their disgusting interests. For $7,000,000 annually, Cuba allowed the United States to use Guantánamo as a naval base, a training camp for the Navy and aviation, and a detention camp for prisoners."

Until 1898, Cuba belonged to Spain. Cuba fought for independence and the United States joined the fight to help its "neighbor." At the end of the war, Spain handed over control of Cuba and other territories, including Puerto Rico, to the United States. In the Platt Amendment of a treaty signed in 1903 and reaffirmed in 1934, the United States recognized Cuba's sovereignty. In return, Cuba granted the

United States complete authority and control over part of its territory through a perpetual rent that could be invalidated only by mutual agreement. When Fidel Castro came to power in 1959, he threatened to remove the Navy base installed in Guantánamo if the United States continued to interfere with the Cuban economy. However, he did not do so because he knew that the United States would use it as a pretext to attack and remove him from power. On January 22, 2009, two days after he was inaugurated as President of the United States, Barack Obama signed an executive order to close the detention camp, stating that the closure would take place in less than a year. Five years later, even though relations with Cuba had improved, the camp remained open. At present, twenty years later, forty prisoners without actual charges of any crime remain detained at Guantánamo.

The young Cortazar had developed a sense of smell for the truth of things and knew that it was the powerful, the bureaucrats, who controlled the course of events. That notion of changing the world, turning it into a holy place, with the same opportunities for everyone, was not an easy thing to accomplish because greed and corruption would never allow such much-desired social change. He said, "Over time, through popular revolts, more than one despot has been pushed out of the way. However, others took power, and history sort of repeated itself. Generally, these men are consumed by greed and possess the ability to plan evil—with a penchant for slaughter. The people had to settle for doing what was human: to half-eat and fight against their imposed misfortune."

The young Cortazar was pursuing a master's degree in Hispanic Literature. He believed that literature was a balm for the ridiculous and absurd human drama. He was head over heels for the work of Julio Cortázar, his literary namesake. He carried a small notebook where he had written down phrases found in the Argentinian writer's books. *"It is not that we must live—since life was given to us. Life lives itself—whether we like it or not,"* he read aloud and asked, "Do you know who said these words?" We all shook our heads, although we knew that the citation was Julio Cortázar's. We were tired of the Cronopio, except Elina, who was entranced looking at the young Cortazar. They admired each other despite their differences. Cortazar was a cautious, compromising, thoughtful young man. On the other hand, Elina, much older, was hasty and held dangerous and radical ideas.

"Just as the Cronopio says, we have no obligation to live," said the reckless woman. "If we want, we can shoot ourselves, and if it were to kill everyone, a bomb would be the solution. A hydrogen bomb would be enough to free the planet from hundreds of thousands of undesirable men and women faster than a rooster crows."

Balzac, biting, punctilious, and always on the offensive (this behavior would eventually lead him to suffer from "Peter the Scaly" syndrome) jumped in to object: "Only a crazy woman can say such nonsense. An atomic weapon was used once and I do not think anyone, any government, would dare to resort to that cruelty, that foolishness, and end up like the Japanese." We thought that, with that observation, he'd muted Elina's mouth, but we were so wrong. Like a fighting cock, Elina returned the attack.

"No, Balzac, here we are talking about beings who are by nature stupid, selfish, and perverse. Once they realized the weapon was effective, they knew for certain that, eventually, they would use it again.

"It seems that you don't know people," she continued. "I've always thought that in *The Creation of Adam*, Michelangelo painted Adam and God pointing at each other not to give each other life, idyllically, but to blame one another, each one trying to force the other to take responsibility for a failed, insane, rotten creation. Adam disdainfully extends his left hand after rebuking him, 'Accept that you screwed up. Look at the botched work you did, genuinely nice everything, but of mediocre quality and perishable. You claim to be omnipotent, the father of the gods, but this crap seems to be made in China.' The other, furious, leaning on his androgynous female side, counterattacks, 'It was your damn guilt, you harassed me with your demands, you wanted a woman like this and that, I lost concentration and, as a result, this world came to be.' The human, full of resentment, retaliates, 'Besides cheap, you are a Machiavellian (Machiavelli was centuries away from being born, but words precede deeds); you attached this unbridled apparatus to us, whose only purpose is to force us to fulfill its damn will to perpetuate and multiply us. And you, quite campy, just disappeared from sight, leaving us all fucked-up.'" We all laughed in celebration of Elina's fantastic invention, thus forgetting all about the Cronopio and the atomic bombs.

In 1998, we left the South Bronx— which, according to Vallejo's stories, *was a place for refugees, literally speaking, because in reality what we had set out to do was to become famous so we could spend our days in bed, but the road was not easy; we usually would only throw flowers at each other's works when read as if in a funeral, until Cortazar showed up and started to fuck our lives up with his literary scissors: 'And you have to cut here and you must cut there, and this is an unnecessary line, and that shall do it, and, see, now it is very nice, and it has an I-don't-know-what, and I do perceive it, though I cannot understand it . . .'*

"The Bonfire," as Elina called the literary workshop, moved to Skármeta's studio on the fifth floor of 62 Canal Street in Lower Manhattan. One of those afternoons of discussions and literary "machetes" came a young man of Mexican descent: Rulfito. His was a new and fun vocabulary: *No manches, culero, órale, chingón, chingada* . . . . Upon hearing him, Cortazar explained that writing is a physiological representation. "Just as various groups of cells take charge of the body's metabolic process, capture O_2 and eliminate CO_2, another group is dedicated to coordinating, integrating, and regulating thoughts, emotions, longings, and other states and reactions that we do not know how to describe." Rulfito's writing was faithful to his language and, by some strange artifice, his texts were a sieve through which the longings for his land, his people, his ancestors, and his gods escaped. His narrative was an authentic representation of his cultural identity.

According to his tales, Rulfito was nourished with the ancestral love of the Aztec god Centéotl and the divine food of tortillas, beans, and nopales that preserved the flavor of earthly fire. Rulfito confessed to feeling happy to be alive despite the bitterness life insisted on making him swallow. Death could be the "cosmic balance," the return to the gods, and the journey to the underworld in the fertile and water-full interior of the earth where life arose—as his Mexican people believed, but he did not. He did not accept such resignation, nor did he want to become another foolish Christ climbing onto a cross, willing to die for anything or anyone. According to the myth, Quetzalcoatl, the god in the shape of a feathered serpent, went down to the underworld and deposited his semen on a pile of bones to give life to man. "A mystical and romantic belief," said Rulfito, "but I am not prepared for death."

He was very young; at only eighteen years old, he did not accept death, which he considered the greatest failure of man. And, as a good "son of the chingada" (that's what he called himself, "a motherfucker-badass" of sorts) with nothing to lose, to ensure he did not end up crippled or a corpse, like thousands of Mexicans, Salvadorans, Guatemalans, and Hondurans, he climbed on "The Beast" or "The Train of Death," rode it until he could ride no more and then, on foot, ran through the desert, climbed walls, and finally arrived where he wanted to be—New York, to make a new life for himself and write stories.

Young Rulfito had a head full of projects he was determined to fight for and to make come true. He was practical and realistic; the hard experiences he had to live through at an early age had taught him that nothing came easy or free. He defined himself as an inhabitant of planet Earth, male, with a lucid mind, and open to possibilities. One of the casual members of the group, who had been a biologist in his country, insisted that the mind was the result of chemical combinations, electrical stimuli, of nerve connections. "Its functioning," the biologist ruled, "depends on the geographical-racial-economic conditions of the individual. The computer-like program installed in the brain's networks is awfully bad if it does not comply with the most optimal stipulations." These comments, which more than theories sounded like vituperations, were taken badly by the whole group.

"Stop *el hueveo*!" Skármeta exclaimed.

"What *vainas* are you saying?" Ureña asked.

"Che, kid, according to your words, here we are all brutes for the mere fact of being Hispanics, poor, brown, and immigrants," chimed in Sabato.

"Scumbag! Come say that crap to my face!" Rulfito screamed at the biologist. "No, no, don't you worry, you don't have to hide or shake like a little girl, I'm not going to hurt you. I'm not even going to insult your little mother. I will only say this to you: Our work will speak for us."

"This is fabulous," Skármeta declared, applauding. "It is in the arena that the roosters are tested!"

"I do not aspire to write three hundred, five hundred pages, but something simple, full of humanity and feeling," Rulfito explained. "Can you imagine writing something like *Pedro Páramo*, the novel by my compatriot Juan Rulfo? *I came to Comala because they told me that my father, a certain Pedro Páramo, lived here. My mother told me.* Are you kidding me?! A short novel written for eternity using the hurting voices of the living and the spectral murmurs of Comala's dead?"

Ureña, the Dominican boy with a radio host's voice, powerful and modulated, interrupted Rulfito. "Me too. Writing short stories for eternity like those of my compatriot Juan Bosch: *Don Damián entered unconsciousness quickly, to the rhythm of the fever that was rising to 104 degrees. His soul felt extremely uncomfortable, almost on the verge of burning, which is why it began to collect in his heart.* What did you think of this small paragraph that is the beginning of the story *The Beautiful Soul of Don Damián*?"

We all remained mute. We seemed to have fallen into a state of enchantment under the influence of his voice.

"Compadre, your voice might as well replace the enchanted flute in *Hamelin*—all of the rats will follow you," said Skármeta, coming out of the spell.

"Leave the flutes and rats to the Brothers Grimm. My voice and my words will sing to love, to the revolution, to the victories of the party, and to the men of good will," exclaimed Ureña, as if he were an actor articulating lines learned by heart.

"Are you kidding me?!" mocked Rulfito. "It seems like the brochures you read have left you a tape recorder for a brain. You are just like a priest repeating every Sunday, every week, every month, and year, the same words: *This is my body and this is my blood.*"

That deep and well-timbered voice of Ureña, more than a budding poet's voice, would have proved perfect for a leader of the masses and for energetic men who made a profession of dumbing down unsuspecting dreamers using incendiary formulas. Despite enjoying the opportunities offered by the capitalist country he chose to live in, Ureña identified as one of these pamphleteering individuals who confused people's right to freedom and happiness with adherence to ideas outside of reality and human possibilities. We did not know the reasons because he never said them. He must have believed that it was fun to run with the sheep of the revolution and not realize how easy it was for the slaughterers to use, as bait, promises of equality and joy for all the men of the earth.

"Don't you realize that you have fallen into the trap of those false prophets who will then tie you all up like chickens and dismember you in the name of a revolution organized for their own interests?" asked N. Malo, a young Cuban who was visiting and spoke from his own experience after crossing ninety miles of a sea full of sharks in a ramshackle *yola* to escape the hell of the revolution.

In response, Ureña, blaming capitalism for the misery of the people—whose benefits he experienced and enjoyed—released those famous verses of Neruda's *Canto General*:

> *Wet flies of humble blood and jam*
> *drunk flies that buzz*
> *on popular graves, circus flies, wise flies*
> *understood in tyranny*

Years passed and Ureña continued to believe in dead people dancing on one leg and continued to believe himself a militant in favor of the cause. What cause? That of living like herded animals and working like oxen, so that the leaders would live like kings? At least that was what he implied, that he was a militant. However, we knew that he lay on the sofa or stayed in bed on days he did not want to work, that he ate in restaurants when he felt like it and invited friends to get drunk on *Brugal*, *Relicario*, or *Matusalem Solera*; we knew he had an SUV (the latest model), an apartment, and that he did not work for someone else. And that was fine.

"Ureña, isn't that what everyone wants?" Skármeta told him as he half-jokingly slapped him on the head. "Stop telling yourself stories and enjoy the life that this 'shitty country,' as you call the United States, offers you."

The Peruvian Vallejo was another serious case—as was the Cuban Arenas. "Compadre, in this group, everyone is a serious case! Revolutions, guerrillas, socialism, communism, and all those crazy doctrines that have fucked up all these assholes! In addition, all these *cabros* are faggots!" exclaimed Skármeta uncorking the third bottle of *Frontera*. Vallejo spoke little, but when he did, it was to curse Alberto Fujimori, Alan García, all the government figures of his country, Mao Tse Tung, Ho Chi Minh, and the Shining Path. According to Skármeta, Vallejo had been a member of the Party, what the Peruvian had called "the only possible party," until they used him as bait and he had to flee to the United States. "Like my fellow university students and intellectuals in my country, I also believed that an active armed movement was necessary to fight against injustice and achieve social transformation, until I realized that this was a dangerous experiment and its results proved horrifying. The use of guerrilla tactics left dead and missing people every day; the movement unleashed some of the bloodiest battles in the history of my country, maybe even of Latin America, in the eighties," said Vallejo.

"Now I understand why Vallejo is taciturn and suspicious," said Malo, the young Cuban guy. "I used to think that I had issues. Long ago, they woke me up. They did it with sticks and bone breakers. Comrades, no one can change the world—not even fix it a little bit. The tyrants are responsible for taking the reins and forcing the world to advance to the rhythm they play, at their whims, crushing and dragging around everyone in the way."

There was resentment and courage in the voices of the comrades Vallejo and Malo, who, like Arenas, had stopped trusting ideologies that forced them to obey as if they were brainless. Now they understood that they had fought for the wrong ends, that the real objective must be to put an end to the system that despised and humiliated human beings, which included putting an end to the communist plague, those who used them for their own benefit and personal interests.

Saddened, Elina approached Vallejo and tried to give him a hug. The Peruvian moved to the side to avoid her. Elina stood still, her arm outstretched, afraid that, when she lowered it, her grief would slip through her fingers. She knew that some of these colleagues considered her incapable of appreciating those things of the spirit that moved humans to perform heroic acts, of understanding the pain of disappointment, of betrayal—much less being able to conceive and create a piece of literature. To relieve resentment and to control those parts of the body that touched the soul weakened her, and she burst into tears in front of those insecure and misogynous fools, blurting out in rage, "You're just well-paid mediocre revolutionaries, hypocrites, traitors. That desire for justice was a pure fairytale, the envy of those at the top. The violence of your actions was nothing but rancor and impotence. If you had been able to change positions with those who oppressed you, you would have done it without a second thought—and then it would have sucked to rub shoulders with the workers, the townspeople, the common man. But, of course, as you could not use any story of heroes and martyrs as a springboard, never mind reach that promised paradise you sought, you arrived in this country, cowering like dogs, with your tails between your legs."

W. Sabines, another Mexican like Rulfito and me, was a guy of few words. He opened his mouth to say only yes or no. Vallejo, his best friend, called him withered and sad, perhaps because he knew that the boy suffered from the sickness of love. Two or three years later, Sabines returned to Mexico, and, over time, very few of us remembered him. Vallejo brought him to mind in one of his stories: *Sabines came up with the idea of telling us that love lasts only four years and I do not know how many months, and I felt like telling him, 'Go to the chingada with that crap!' But the withered fellow suffocated us with his chemical and chimerical explanations.* Elina never had a chance to chat with him because Sabines never gave her the opportunity to do so, and she wanted to speak to him even less after she heard him talking to Vallejo about her, "This woman, like any other woman, does not show any talent. She writes some nonsense just to get the writing out of the way. If she sneaked into this group, it was to get herself a macho."

Sometime later, when the group had disintegrated and only Elina, Skármeta, Balzac, and I still got together, she confessed to us the reason for her erratic behavior. On occasion, she was dull. Other times, she was haughty, and often aggressive and sarcastic.

When she joined the writers' club, she had been leaving some difficult moments behind: a broken relationship, the loss of her business and her home, and her children suffering her emotional and financial instability. She was vulnerable. Things as simple as seeing a bird fly or a leaf fall from a tree put her to death. "That's why I ended up crying when I read my writings: emotions and the feeling of failure strangled me. I had fallen. I felt crushed by the teeth of misfortune, just like that son devoured by Saturn in Goya's painting. I did not want anyone's compassion, and yet I could not control myself, and I offered that ridiculous spectacle giving others the pleasure of seeing me defeated and crying." Time shut our mouths. As Balzac said in defense of Elina, "She was not in the group to get a macho; rather, she was with us after having pushed a man out of her life, for she had stopped loving him and saw in us, not males, but a gang of crazy dreamers with whom she could start living her own dreams."

Never imagining that in the future we would have to praise Elina's work, we made fun of her. We scoffed when she talked about the methods of thought, the nuances of the spirit, and human passions. As if she had a capacity for reflection or possessed the gift for philosophical reasoning! Reluctantly, out of commitment or because they were the rules of the group, we had no choice but to listen to her elucubrations that pretended to be great. "Every day one does the same thing: gets up in the morning, goes to the bathroom, urinates, brushes their teeth, showers, has breakfast, goes to work, and returns home just to perform and repeat the same tasks as always. However, one day comes along that is different. That day one realizes that one is alive and wonders why one is alive, what the meaning of life is, and the reason for our existence. For the first time, one realizes that being alive means that, one day or another, sooner or later, one will die, and that there is no way out, no way around it, and then: one great wave of panic. That is the human drama. I find that the only option we have to prevent ourselves from going crazy or committing suicide is *not to think*. Do not think. Try to be happy by overcoming difficulties as best you can, even if the shadow of the inevitable haunts you at every step."

"Let her say *hueváas*, but do not listen to her. She's at her worst when she thinks she's Einstein and smothers us with concepts she thinks she can manage. As if relativity, quantum mechanics, or black holes were the same as changing her panties. All because she studied engineering—which she's had little use for because she simply took the wrong path. The poor 'cabrita' cannot even tell a nail from a screw," Skármeta declared.

Cortazar was enthusiastic about this labyrinth of complicated concepts: "We are here. We are a part of this crazy world. Since we do not understand it, let's talk about it to see if we untangle the skein." According to his own bestiary, Cortazar authored stories born of his Cortázar's readings that were not supposed to touch any enigmatic facet of "the everyday" (dodging a fall into metaphysics), but just like his favorite writer, he was in search of the deeper sense of reality. "I want to understand how and why atomic particles do not have a certain position or a certain velocity, but many, simultaneously," Cortazar said, intrigued.

"Come on, Elina, you who think you know it all, how do you get out of that one?!" Vallejo jumped in with a mocking tone.

She, enjoying the moment, replied, "Matter is dynamic and not entirely predictable. Therein lies the principle of uncertainty. One simple example is the flight of a fly. We chase her to kill her, right? But, sometimes, we think the damn thing might be magical because it disappears from our visual field. The fly is still flying in the room; however, we do not manage to control all of its locations due to its speed. We can only locate its position when it stops or slows down."

Vallejo went to the window and took a look at the street from the fifth floor where Skármeta's studio was, perhaps because he would not accept that or any other answer from the pedantic Ecuadorian. Outside, on Canal Street, Manhattan's Chinatown, where they gathered every Saturday, hundreds of people walked in all directions, surrounded by restaurants with roast ducks hanging in stained glass windows and trinket shops for tourists from all over the world. Angrily, he said to himself, "The principle of uncertainty, that matter is dynamic; everything is in constant motion."

To his misfortune, Cortazar continued to wind up Elina and she was pleased to go on with her speech because, well, she loved to be the center of attention—repeatedly resorting to tears to get it. The group had welcomed a couple of other women—females as God intended, nice women, attractive, without those airs of I-know-it-all. Vallejo could not stand Elina to the point of doubting that she was indeed a female. He could not imagine her coming on to a man, causing him an erection, screaming, or actually having sex with anyone. How and when did she mother those two children she claimed to have? What kind of man could be interested in a woman who could not elicit a single sexual thought?

We heard Cortazar's insisting voice, "I do not know about you, but I've always been intrigued to know about things that are hard to understand. For example, I heard in a documentary that there is order in chaos and anarchy; that this phenomenon can be seen in different situations and systems, including the universe."

"Let me offer you some examples so that you can understand that paradox," Elina interrupted. Vallejo, still by the window, heard her and thought about leaving before the speech began because he was about to vomit. "In physics, that chaotic state is known as entropy. Now, let us see how this contradictory concept works:

disorder brings order. Imagine that we put oranges in a basket and shake them all up; that is, we scramble them around. We know this action is an example of chaos, however, when we look at the oranges, we can see that they have fallen, spontaneously, into a certain sort of order . . ."

"If entropy is disorder, how can one speak of balance?" Balzac interrupted Elina now—he enjoyed putting her on the spot.

"I'm going to explain this to you in an effortless way, so that even a mental cripple could understand," Elina said with a mocking smile. "If coffee, milk, and sugar are mixed in a cup, a chaotic state is achieved which, nonetheless, maintains the balance of the three distinct elements in a single substance, a process that is also irreversible because the three elements cannot be separated again."

Hearing these last words, Vallejo touched his forehead, believing he had a fever. Elina's petulance bothered him.

Worse yet, to see how Cortazar and Rulfito celebrated everything that came out of this insufferable woman's mouth. Time passed and many, in addition to Vallejo and Balzac, were surprised when her books—like *Beyond Infinite, Order and Chaos,* or *Another Space*— were published. They could not believe Elina had dared to use these concepts to create stories and, least of all, that she had the writing ability to do so. Very much to our regret, we had to accept that she'd done very well. When *"The Forbidden Dream"* won a short story prize in Spain, as a compliment, Balzac sarcastically told her that she was "a successful failure." The oxymoron fell like a poisoned dart on her chest, but aware of the acidic personality of "Mr. No Concessions," she faked a smile. It was not that Elina was gifted when it came to transferring her emotions to paper or scrutinizing people's minds or hearts to transform their passions and longings into short stories and novels. None of that. What happened was that Elina was malicious and manipulative, and she used the art of the written word to criticize and condemn society, show the dark side of people, skin half the world, and get rid of those who made her swallow poison with their ill-intended words and actions. Her characters enjoyed death, killed for revenge, and were never willing to forgive—not even those who lay underground.

Elina believed in conspiracy theories. No one could convince her that there was not an organization made up of individuals who controlled wealth, monopolized the sources of production, manipulated commercial programs, banks, and global economic operations, commanded the intelligence services, and even regulated the birth rate required for each era. The entire world responded to their demands, she thought, and the governments of the planet feared them, even though no one knew them. It could be the Rothschilds, the Rockefellers, the Morgans, or the Bushes, no one could say who exactly. What was known was what Nathan Rothschild declared one day: *I do not care which puppet occupies the British throne to rule the empire where the sun never sets. The man who controls England's monetary resources controls the British Empire, and I control those resources.*

"You're full of shit, sheer *hueváas*," warned Skármeta (not too far from such violent action himself), and we all laughed. "I do not understand how you dare to say all this crap, unafraid that one day someone will punch your teeth out." Elina, without a trace of feeling intimidated or self-conscious, went on.

"You laugh because you do not know the extent of the Machiavellian minds of these individuals. These monsters discovered that wars were profitable, so they invested fortunes in them. If you do some research, you will know that Senator and banker Prescott Bush was suspected of profiting from World War II by establishing big business with the companies that financed Hitler's government. Guys, you are naïve. You use your shit phones, those cordless ones that are fashionable now (digital phones were not yet in use nor were navigation devices or GPS), unaware that they receive signals from a space station, which is nothing more than a surveillance center. And that is not a joke or story, nor is the cyber program story, where very soon it will be possible to enter all the information about a person and then predict what he or she will do in the future. You will see soon enough. Then they will install it on satellites placed in space with all the data needed to stalk and manipulate human activity, as well as the world political state."

"Now Elina will tell us that the gringos never made it to the moon or that Christopher Columbus and his crew were Jews," Balzac said, stretching out one of his famous sardonic grimaces. Rulfito, for what it was worth, applauded enthusiastically, encouraging her to tell another of those stories that, because they were not confirmed by an expert or a researcher, became mere speculation. And yet, for example, biblical tales were to be taken at face value when everyone knew these were beliefs that could not be verified experimentally.

"Of course, Balzac, the gringos reached the moon, don't you think so? Remember that following the war more than one thousand German scientists were moved to the United States. One of those scientists was Wernher von Braun, 'Father of the American lunar program.' He was the chief engineer of the Saturn V super heavy-lift launch vehicle that propelled the Apollo spacecraft to the Moon. Don't tell me you think the pyramids were the work of aliens. Human ingenuity makes the unimaginable possible!

"And yes, exactly, Columbus and his crew were Jewish. Sephardim 'converts,' as the Spanish Jews were known, who converted to Christianity to escape death. 'Conversion or death,' this could be read on a sign placed in the squares of the Iberian Peninsula of the time," Elina said—she was sure of it all because she had just read it in a book or heard it on some television program titled *The Truth Is Before Your Eyes* or some such. "Probably this data was hidden by racism, by discrimination, or, as it is said now, by anti-Semitism—when Arabs are as Semitic as Jews. It was not intended to recognize the Jews as the first to arrive in the Americas, to give credence to those who were considered the heirs of Christ's murderers. Perhaps the historians of the time were also Jews and feared that the Inquisition would pursue them to the New World."

Skármeta could not stand it when someone else took over a conversation and spitefully said, "If we were at the time of the Inquisition, you would surely end up burned at the stake for speaking so much *hueváa*."

Elina ignored him and continued talking: "In 1492, the Catholic monarchs Isabella and Ferdinand sought to soften the political, social, economic, and religious tensions caused by the hatreds and resentments that aroused the power and influence of the Jews, so they signed an edict ordering the expulsion of the Hebrews from their territories. The monarchs were convinced that the courts of the Inquisition, created years earlier, would accuse and punish the Jews who had converted to Christianity to save themselves. Most Sephardim chose to leave, abandoned their goods, and lost their money, not only trying to escape from the threats against their lives in Spain but in search of new horizons and to be able to keep their faith in their beliefs and traditions."

According to Elina's stories, Petrarca "Petita" Torres (her maternal grandmother) said—as she smoked her smelly cigar—that the crew hoped to reach lands where they spoke Hebrew, so during the first voyage of Columbus they brought Luis Torres as a translator. But her ancestor was not Luis Torres, who died along with the thirty-eight other men that the admiral left on the island called La Española, but Antonio Torres. Antonio was a Sephardic native of

Extremadura who in 1493 embarked to the New World during the second voyage commanded by Columbus, another Sephardic. According to Elina, the story told at school, and which everyone accepted without question, was not true. Queen Isabella did not offer any jewels to raise funds for the trip to any Indies, as legend has it, nor could she afford to offer money because the royal treasury was exhausted during the war against the Moors.

"It was the important and wealthy Jews such as Gabriel Sánchez, treasurer of the kingdom of Aragon, and Luis de Santangel, scribe of the same kingdom, who paid for the project and offered the three ships for the trip, convinced that they would find in 'the other land' the ten lost Hebrew tribes as indicated by the prophecies of Isaiah: *For, behold, I am going to create new heavens and a new earth.* Cristóbal Colón (Christopher Columbus) and not Cristoforo Colombo was the name of the admiral. History presented him as 'Genovese' to confuse the world and not call him 'Marrano,' which at that time was another of the nicknames given to the Sephardim. And to continue with the farce, and hide his Hebrew origin, dangerous and suspicious at that time, it was said that he was Castilian, Italian, Portuguese, and even Greek. However, notes, minutes, and letters of the admiral were written in Spanish and not in Italian, for Spanish was his native language. It was striking that in his correspondence he did not use the word Jesus and yet spoke of the Lord and quoted biblical names such as Israel, David, and Judah, which reveals his knowledge of the Old Testament. The letters addressed to his son Diego are perhaps the clearest confirmation of his origins. In these, in the upper left-hand corner, there were Hebrew letters. Also, on the margin of a random page in one of his books, although the year was 1481, he wrote 5241, the date of the Jewish calendar."

When Elina finished her story, we were all impressed. All we had left was to look at one another. What she had just narrated sounded convincing and logical, even when we knew that apocryphal tales could not be trusted, nor could conspiracy theories. We were all convinced that anyone who deviated from the rules of the history textbooks, and did not know how to distinguish between what should and should not be said, was crazy.

That is why none of us were surprised when, in 1998, we learned that Elina was held for three days in the asylum.

"Her wires were peeled!" Vallejo exclaimed.

"What wires or *hueváas*?" Skármeta squawked. "The 'cabra' was always crazy! I figure she told one of her crazy stories and was taken away by the madmen's guards."

"Umm, they should have left her locked up for a few months so that this fool could learn her lesson and not continue fucking with us," Balzac added.

Rulfito, knowing of the difficult moments his friend was going through, said, "Now we can say that Elina possesses a divine gift. She is not crazy, she is just a little wacko and totally ungodly. Elina has shown us she has the guts to do and say whatever she wants without caring about ending up at the psychiatrist. 'Chingones,' we feel envy, we cannot deny it. We would all like to be compared to wonderful crazy people like Edgar Allan Poe, Virginia Woolf, or the hallucinating Tolstoy."

What amazed us the most about Elina's horrible experience was the comments she made about God, which helped get her into serious trouble: "I am not worried about divine existence, but the absence of evidence. Whether God exists or not, knowing how and where he came from is what interests me. *Something* had to cause *its* existence." Elina told us that the doctor responded that God was necessary and eternal. He did not require an external cause to exist—the cause was himself, to which she replied, "We can say the same about the universe. Why think of God if we can assume that the universe was necessary and eternal and caused itself?" As if that were not enough, she commented that quantum theory had shown that not everything obeys the laws of physics: there are random processes, impossible to predict, that follow the rules of, say, roulette. "God does play dice," she said, mocking Einstein, and continued, "The quantum factor shows that consciousness plays an essential role in physical reality; the atomic world is only materialized when an observer is aware of it."

"That's nonsense," the doctor had said. "The world exists whether we observe it or not."

"Perhaps we are within the universe that our mind perceives as reality," she replied. "In another world, you might be the patient."

Elina said this and that, and to her surprise, she saw the doctor lift the headset and ask for assistance. In no time, Elina found out that she could no longer back down. She had said things in front of an insensitive and ignorant person about notions essential to her—things he found improper. In a matter of minutes, she was inside a cage, covered only by a white robe, without her eight earrings and the thousand bracelets that always accompanied her.

Elina could be locked in a cage for repeating foolishness; however, that did not seem to matter to her because she didn't complain. Elina needed to question each and every imposed truth. Skeptical, she continued to argue that the heinous terrorist attacks on September 11, 2001 were not perpetrated by trained foreign men on American soil. She said, "The extremist Muslim groups Al-Qaeda, the Taliban Islamic movement, and Osama bin Laden possibly had nothing to do with the fall of the World Trade Center towers."

Skármeta contradicted her angrily. "That is another of the *huenáas* that you repeat over and over, another of the petty and perverse conspiracies that only crazy people like you can believe. From my window, here on Canal Street, I saw the planes of the terrorists crashing into the towers."

"So what? The fact that you saw the planes does not mean that the Muslims were responsible. Anyone could have flown the planes! Where are the bodies to prove it?"

Supporting the theory defended by his admired friend, Rulfito intervened, "Let us think reasonably. The fuel tanks of the planes could not produce the heat needed to melt the steel structures of those tremendous buildings."

"That is correct," Elina insisted, emboldened by the support of her partner. "The crash of the planes was only part of the theater to cover up the controlled demolition, to have sufficient reason to start the war in the Gulf; or perhaps it served to destroy evidence that the government didn't know how to eliminate."

Skármeta, pouting as if he were a big, dumb child, said, "Now you want to invent other *hueváas*! I, like thousands of conscious citizens, supported the government's decision to invade Afghanistan and then Iraq. We had a moral obligation to punish the real culprits. That is the truth, there is no other." Skármeta, with a triumphant voice, ended the discussion.

Elina looked at him with a grudge, challenging him with her gaze. She looked like a snake standing on a rock ready to attack, but she calmed down and decided not to continue with the dispute. She even felt pity for that fearful old man.

"Please stop talking about the attacks," cried el Cubano, N. Malo. "That horrible day I was supposed to die with the rest of my co-workers, most of them immigrants like me. I used to work at

Windows on the World, the restaurant on the 106th floor in the North Tower. That September 11, I was drunk and didn't go to work. I feel guilty, I escaped death while so many people died."

The thing did not stop there, though, because Vallejo, with a pitiful voice, announced, "Remember that I am one of the victims of the terrorist attack. This tumor that recently stretched out of my head was the result of the toxins I was exposed to that fateful morning. That September 11th, I was present at the disaster. I swear that just before the towers collapsed, like hundreds of people, I heard the din of a bomb exploding. That was a work of self-destruction."

Upset, his best friend, the Mexican Sabines, told him to shut up—lest those statements come out of those walls and get Vallejo in trouble. Vallejo had once been accused of having participated in the clashes against the government of Alberto Fujimori—as a member of the *Shining Path*, the Peruvian communist guerrilla group that followed the lines of Marxism-Leninism and Maoism. Vallejo, unaware of the royal mess he could get into, one day had told us:

"I was supposed to never agree with Alberto.
'Who is Alberto?' we all asked.
Who else could Alberto be other than that little man who governed us, who governed them, I mean; because I got off that bus a long time ago to come here. Because New York is New York. Here I assumed the status of a mental refugee . . ."

To put an end to the dangerous exchange, Sabato, with a tango voice, said, "Let's get to the matter at hand and leave all this nonsense behind. Let's read."

As a teenager, H. Sabato had come from the pampas, Corrientes 348 or The Esquina Rosada. The young man was willing, if necessary, to cross on a donkey's back from the Bronx to Manhattan if his verses had a chance to be heard anywhere from here to Patagonia, at the very end of the world. We did not see him again for a few years and, when we found him, we realized that time, with its vines and brambles, had made the boy, now a mature man, add the rules of mysticism to his repertoire of beautiful words. The poet, on his way to becoming a hermit, said, "I do not want to extend a wait devoid of real expectation. All of us have been part of a dark generation with no intention of knowing the mysteries of life. The horizon is not the end of the road. Beyond that line, other horizons await. I want to help you find that path of liberation where suffering and dissatisfaction can end through the abandonment of desires."

All of us who participated in the group at that time looked at each other in surprise, wondering if Sabato had fallen ill and was getting ready to leave this world, at peace with life. Already that poem, written in youth, which we celebrated so much, predicted his dissatisfaction with the world around us:

Today I need to change the course of events
and among other things raise my guard
to the canary,
forget the sack of words on my back,
leave for the Moon in search of food,
travel by donkey from the Bronx to
Manhattan . . .

"This *huevón* can very well go to the other world, but don't come fuck with us with those *hueváas*," Skármeta complained as usual.

"*Mayimbe*, Che querido, you must have made a wrong turn or something," said the poet Ureña. "Go back to wherever you came from because here we do not want you to fix our lives. We want no consolations or *vainas raras*."

Elina added, "I got off that skateboard a long time ago. The mysteries of the divine kingdom, I'll leave them to the enlightened. I have already gone through that stage of search and mysticism. Right now, I am proud of my humanity, tied to matter, conscientiously reveling in the joys and enduring the sorrows of each day, fighting arm-in-arm to continue in this: my wonderful world of crap."

"What do you think of all this *hueváa*?" Skármeta asked Balzac, who, as always, avoiding compromise, took refuge with his favorite saying of the closed mouth and the flies. We all berated him because we were angry at his so-called prudence. Unable to find a way out, he said, "Meditation and yoga relax me. Just like you, I would like to know what I came to this world for, but then the struggle for survival makes me forget what I was looking for. As Honoré de Balzac said: *All happiness depends on courage and work. I have had many periods of misery, but with energy and above all with illusions, I surpassed them all.* Which I translate as 'Happiness is found in good purpose, in daily life, in strength, and tenacity to overcome evil.'"

"In other words," Elina said by taking the words away from Balzac, "whoever lives on illusions or thinks they can abandon the fight for life through meditation instead of grabbing the bull by the horns, should go ahead and do it. Although you should know that you are lying because that is impossible; the only way to escape from yourself is through hanging yourself by the neck and thus remain still forever."

Ureña intervened, "Now, let Sabato believe he is Buddha and pretend to take us to Nirvana or whatever that mystical state is called."

Surprising us, Balzac added: "It seems to me that we must respect his ideas. Those who believe and feel like Sabato may follow him."

"We do not know the reasons for his transformation and search," Elina said. "Probably his writings embittered him—he discovered that those worlds he invented in books resembled the real world too much and he looked for another way out. That probably happened to Sabato." She continued, "His responsibility as a writer forced him to show reality. Although with the word we disguise, transform, and even embellish the most terrible things, we cannot hide their true essence. That would have the same effect as attempting to disguise the stink of shit with perfume. Life is what it is. We wallow in its misery. Humans are just like those rats that run the rails of the subways."

Vallejo waited for Elina to stop talking and then said, "Sometimes you feel like escaping, to give meaning to life. One resists being a different animal, an animal that eats and gathers because the laws of nature demand it, a miserable animal that one day receives its death with no knowledge that all has come to an end."

"That is understandable," Elina said. "As Camus says: *Any man, around any corner, can experience the feeling of the absurd because everything is absurd.* . . . Sabato has found himself in that trance. In order not to blow his brains out, he's sought relief in that other world promised by mystics."

Looking up, as a response, I repeated one of my famous phrases, "The drop fell, the ant died."

Applauding my intervention, Elina continued, "What a pity to have life and spend it on meditations, prayers, and bullshit! That doesn't sit well with me. As I understand it, the bitter chalice, the cross, and the bleating of a wounded goat were already suffered by a Christ to bequeath us a more bearable life, more proper for . . ."

"Shhh," Skármeta hissed, so that we found an end to our ongoing tinkering. "Let's stop this *hueváa* and move our music elsewhere."

With time, several of the regular members of the group moved away for different reasons. Sabines returned to Mexico, Cortazar got a job as a professor of languages at a university in another state, and Sabato formed his own group. The rest of us continued to meet sporadically. Not so Elina, Skármeta, and Balzac, who met regularly in one of the Chilean's apartments in the vicinity of Central Park West. All three were masochists because they well knew they could hurt each other with words, especially if they had more than two drinks. Despite the encounters and tantrums, they went through with it because of their difficult and passionate personalities, and the three cultivated a close friendship, even traveling together to other countries.

After a while, Balzac began to suffer anxiety attacks accompanied by feverish and manic states, probably because of the political crisis and economic collapse in his country.

According to estimates made by the United Nations, in recent years, more than two million Venezuelans crossed the border with Colombia, fleeing from the worst economic crisis in the country's recent history, with the highest inflation rate in the world and with problems of shortages of certain foods, medicines, and basic products. Experts said the problem stemmed from the external debt crisis and prolonged economic instability in the 1980s, due to the global drop in oil prices. Inflation soared in 1996 and poverty rates increased.

In 1998, Hugo Chávez was elected president. Socialist, anti-imperialist, and influenced by the theory of equitable distribution of wealth, Chávez initiated the so-called "Bolivarian Revolution." This movement, created to help the people and support countries that lacked oil resources, increased public spending and increased foreign debt in an uncontrolled manner. Years later, the reduction of incomes, the increase in imports, the decline in national production, as well as corruption and excessive public spending, were cited as factors that led the country to hyperinflation, economic depression, shortages of basic products, and a drastic increase in unemployment, poverty, malnutrition, diseases, infant mortality, and crime.

In the 2006 presidential election, Chávez was re-elected. He then announced that he would push his political projects through reforms to the Constitution, including taking control of the Armed Forces, new economic regulations, and indefinite re-election. Chávez was re-elected for a third consecutive term in 2012, but, because he died in March 2013 from complications of colon cancer, new elections were held that April, in which Vice President Nicolás Maduro was elected, granting continuity to the so-called "Bolivarian Revolution." The results of the presidential election in 2014 triggered a series of demonstrations associated with the economic crisis, the increase in crime rates nationwide, and allegations of corruption in public bodies. One day, Venezuelans, desperate in the face of the crisis, started the inevitable mass exodus.

Knowing that the Venezuelan nation had at some point enjoyed times of wealth, thanks to owning the largest oil reserves in the world, and yet now his people wandered the roads of neighboring countries in search of shelter and food—destitute, so to speak—caused an emotional imbalance in Balzac's already affected psyche. We feared that he would suffer a crisis while teaching one of his classes and be forced to resign. Worried, we couldn't find a way to confront and convince him to seek psychological help before worse things happened to him. How to approach him without him taking the advice wrong and reacting badly? How could we ask him what was wrong? How could we tell him that his behavior was strange, that it was difficult to spend time with him? One day, as naturally as can be, Elina, without preamble, recommended that he go to a doctor she knew because she found him worried and distant. Balzac confessed to suffering from insomnia and agreed to seek the professional's help. It seems that the evils were more than one because Balzac became a mobile pharmacy with a number of pills and medical supplies he began to carry in a backpack.

In July 2018, Elina and Balzac traveled to Ecuador. Elina had arranged the presentation of one of her novels at a university. Miguel, a common friend, joined them in Guayaquil so the three could enjoy the trip without worrying that he would have a bad time. Miguel told us how things happened. Balzac had thought the trip would be a good opportunity to also present a literary magazine where the three of them were part of the editorial team. The day before the event, the person in charge informed Elina that only the novel could be presented. They were at a meal offered by Elina's cousins when she broke the news to them.

That was enough for Balzac to suffer one of his crises, throwing a tantrum and screaming his lungs out uncontrollably. Elina did not have the opportunity to tell them that she, as usual, did not intend to respect any regulation imposed by anyone and the presentation of the book and the magazine would go as planned, and that would be the end of the story. With his soul plagued by rage, Balzac gave free rein to his demons and attacked Elina, after he had already verbally assaulted a colleague back in the U.S. Part of his personality, rather than his illness, was resentment . . . and revenge. "You'll see, I will sabotage the presentation for you," he said, rabid, as if the words were poisoned darts, while he cornered himself in the back of the courtyard, refusing to take a bite of food.

Those were the facts. These things happened the way they did, but it is difficult to say the real motives that would cause Balzac to act in such an explosive and disloyal way. Elina was smarter and more poisonous than Balzac though. She could have retaliated with far more offensive things, screwing up secrets that she knew of him, plunging him into the despair of his insecurities and weaknesses, but she decided to overlook the offense, knowing the health problem that Balzac was going through. They were friends—and that feeling, born between two beings, was a kind of luck that entailed responsibilities and, at that moment, at least one of them was aware of that involuntary, strange, disinterested bond that takes form in the human heart and stands beyond selfishness and insults. Trying to find an excuse for her friend's outburst, Elina said that surely it was not easy for the Venezuelan to see his compatriots selling soft drinks and knick-knacks in the streets, asking for handouts on public transport, prostituting themselves on street corners.

But back in New York, the issues continued. We all read the offensive, damaging comments against whom we all thought was his friend because Balzac used social media to make them. When Elina asked him to apologize for the irrational behavior he displayed in front of her family, Balzac replied, "It wasn't in front of your family, only your cousin, who has ties to organized crime and has a thief for a husband." Elina told us that she could not believe these statements came from her friend. She needed to reread them to be able to assimilate them. She decided not to delete them, to keep them on the computer as a reminder of those painful moments. So affected and out of reality was the Venezuelan, he did not realize he was betraying the trust his friend had given him and was behaving like a miserable scoundrel. Not satisfied with defaming a person who treated him with respect and had kindly offered to show him the city, but attempting also to completely destroy *her,* Balzac sought out Skármeta. Who knows with what intrigues, he managed to get the Chilean on his side. Skármeta, also using social networks, warned her never to approach him again under threat of going to the police and asking for a restraining order. Elina felt hurt; another of her friends turned his back on her and without even knowing the facts, without having listened to her version of the story before deciding. Unheard of! Skármeta was worried about his safety? As if he hadn't known her for more than twenty years! Elina, incredulous still and grief-stricken, re-read Skármeta's words: "If you were able to hit Balzac, what would you do to me, a poor old man?"

At that time, Elina was learning a lesson—whether she wanted to or not. She had to admit that the people she appreciated wouldn't always appreciate her the same. She had to suffer the betrayals and infidelities of those around her; she had to endure them because she shared this world with selfish, jealous, envious beings, capable of all evil passions. The noblest and most disinterested relationship that can exist between human beings was being destroyed by a moment of delirium. But this was the human being: intelligence and knowledge served him little in the face of his nature and egotism. To go guilt-free, Balzac hid in what he called "wounded dignity" and brazenly dared to write, "However, I already forgave you because I think you didn't know what you were doing."

More than a year later, when Balzac had, in part, regained emotional stability, he approached Elina. She decided to leave behind those bad times—with doubts, of course, if this had been at all a true friendship. "What is friendship?" She wondered. "It is certainly a noble and selfless relationship, but what does it mean? What does it feel like?" She always believed that the person she chose as a friend would support her in everything and at every moment without expecting anything in return. She was given the confidence with the assurance that she could count on it. From the beginning, it is known that this friend is a person, who, as such, has defects; and yet, he or she is accepted without conditions. So, why did she feel sad and disappointed when that person failed her and betrayed her trust? "Could it be that I demanded too much from Balzac?" She knew that he was a distrustful and insecure person who used irony to protect a wounded ego. "I offered him my friendship precisely because I thought he needed someone to lean on," Elina told me.

On any given day, Elina thought that she and Balzac could be friends again and leave behind both the resentment and disappointment. They attended a meeting of friends they had in common and, without mentioning what happened, they reconnected once again. After all, they were no longer the young people who met at the end of the century, but a couple of old people who traveled a long way together. However, as Elina confessed to me, even though she and Balzac were fully aware of their human imperfections and that, without the need for words, they promised not to hurt each other again or betray their friendship, she felt that something had broken and that things would never be like the old days.

"It has occurred to me to kill you. The problem is that I still can't find a proper way." That was the message Vallejo sent to Elina one day through the social networks.

"That's the best compliment I've ever received in my life," she replied. "I love that you want to kill me. I like the phrase so much that I'm going to borrow it to include in my next novel." Vallejo and Elina did not know how or when they had become friends and, at this point in life, it no longer made sense to investigate the details. Not surprisingly, more than two decades had passed since we all had arrived at "The Bonfire," that literary workshop in the South Bronx. Now both, like the rest, had aged. We all had wrinkles and scars caused by the low blows life had given us. Over time, Elina and the Peruvian Vallejo had understood that what separated them was insignificant, even vulgar. Vanity, selfishness, envy, all those destructive passions faded over the years. Now they looked back and their disagreements seemed like the stuff of children.

"Dear, do you know I dreamed that you told me you were going to use my words in one of your novels? I've decided to write a story about that dream. I'll send it to you as soon as it's finished so you can find out the method I used to remove you." Elina and Vallejo laughed like two children celebrating their antics. She with her hands on her hips hurting from osteoporosis, he enduring the ravages that cancer had left him in the spine caused by the toxic materials released that 9/11 when New York was the target of terrorist attacks.

"Vallejo, don't. In this story, you are killing your friends!" said Sabato, dying of laughter. "At first, it was dedicated to Elina, but I thought it was better to kill several birds with one stone," said Vallejo. We were gathered in a café in Queens in support of Vallejo, after learning of his cancer. It was good for us to support each other. We did not deceive ourselves; we all suffered from one ailment or another. We were a bunch of pathetically funny old people who brought out pains and ills without any shame. The same way things happened to every human being out there, some good, some terrible, we had crossed the path of the years until we reached the moment of accepting reality and confessing that, like any miserable living being, our bodies had surrendered; there was no other way and no other body. We also knew that, if something—a person, a memory, a desire, a goal—remained latent in our minds, in our souls, we would still be overflowing with desire for life. Not expecting anything, neither good nor bad, that was true old age.

"What has become of Skármeta's life that we haven't seen him or heard from him again for so long?" Rulfito asked. Vallejo replied that the last time he heard from him, in his own words, he had been kidnapped in Chile.

"Crazy old man who makes up stories to keep feeling important!" Ureña exclaimed. "And talking about crazy old people, why isn't Elina with us? Don't tell me our beloved friend and sister has already stretched her legs in a coffin," Ureña asked, half-joking.

Evidently hurt, Balzac gave us the news. He said that just that morning, he learned from Elina's sister that our friend was in the hospital. "No one knows yet what happened to her. She is unconscious. And look at us, we talk about death and how to kill friends."

"We are *culeros,* sons of the *chingada,*" said Rulfito, and we all shook our heads from one side to the other, refusing to believe that Elina was prostrated in a bed, unable to argue, without the strength to protest this or that.

Vallejo said that we had to resign ourselves to the idea that, perhaps, Elina would not come back to us, and the only thing left was to pray for the salvation of her soul.

Angry, Rulfito said, "Don't say those *chingaderas!* You know Elina did not believe in those tales of souls, paradises, and hells invented by fucking tricksters. Also, I'm sure Elina is going to recover."

We remained silent for a long time, feeling that words were useless to drive away grief. Paradoxically, the possibility of death, and its closeness, led us to reflect on life. Unable to avoid it, we thought about how unstable and ephemeral our journey through this world was. What good were intelligence and achievements? What gain is there in all our pride if in the end, we will reach a point where everything is reduced to dust, to ashes? How important are life and death for humanity, and for the universe? We said goodbye. We hugged, grateful to have crossed paths and become friends.

"We're going to miss that crazy woman," Sabato said.

"That crazy one we love so much," Rulfito added.

I wake up. It feels like I have slept for years. I am tired and dazed. With my eyes still closed, I hear the noises that come from outside—confused with the murmur produced by the beating of my heart, the flow of blood through my veins, and the crossing of thoughts through my brain. No, those are not my thoughts, those are my memories digging into my consciousness. What happened to me? I started rolling around the world carrying my passions and miseries, the others assaulted me, I attacked back, I lost the fight, I ended up lying on the floor like a wounded animal, I stood up to go on my way, I wanted to kill those responsible for my pain, I went crazy.

I always knew that the day would come when that nightmare of mine would come true. I walked into a room and found myself waiting for *me*. It was like observing myself from the other side of a mirror. I thought I was prepared and had everything in order so that I would not have to be accountable to anyone. Deluded. That was not possible. How can one be ready for this moment if one does not even know what the hell one is doing in this life? Debts, claims, and settling of accounts were still outstanding. The children, the friends, the whole world demanded answers. It was hypocritical and cowardly to declare that one did not regret anything. How to declare such a lie if there is always something that one wishes had not happened? How to leave the past behind if the mind is inflexible and returns us, again and again, to the unfortunate moments from which one would like to escape? There are things I regret and others I would commit again a thousand times. I regret not killing the damned bastard with my bare hands. They were saved from my revenge and my justice because painfully this country does not accept the law of the talion: *an eye for an eye and a tooth for a tooth*. My childish mind forgot an unfortunate fact, but it did not forget that I was capable of sending a beast that caused harm to the other world. I had seen how Dad got rid of the rats that entered the house by putting the poison in the food he left for them, and I knew I could do the same with that scumbag we called Grandfather. He didn't die; I regret not putting enough of the 1080 in his oat drink. I didn't manage to kill that rat, but I had the pleasure of watching him convulse on the floor—his eyes wide like open gates, bloodshot, just about to burst. My mom's half-siblings almost killed her: they blamed her for the gross spectacle, yet I didn't open my mouth. I knew my mother was suspicious of me, so I was sent to the nuns to have their teachings draw the devil out of my soul.

So many things happened, mistakes and failures, that they were left behind until it was time to respond. Everyone who was offended demanded reparations and cried out for justice and revenge. One sees oneself cornered and hides behind the imperfect human nature that leads one to commit barbarities. One asks for kindness, and understanding, even though, one knows that, within our human hearts, passions burn, with too much resentment, too much rancor. By what right can one expect from others something different if the same passions burn all of us within our chests? If the past could be erased, if only the good could be rescued from yesterday. But life does not allow those graces: nothing can be erased—and it will be so until the day of our death.

Keeping memories alive: that's life's secret, its power, its pleasure. Some speak of a divine judgment after death. That's another fallacy. That judgment is of this world where remorse, guilt, and sorrow inflame and wound the human mind and heart—without the slightest need for the flames of hell. That judgment has no place or time, it may come at any time in life. Because it is essential to being alive, only in this way can a person responsible for everything that remains to be elucidated be able to answer before the only judge there will ever be: oneself. Oneself and one's memories. No one else. There are faults of which one is not guilty. What happened was the result of human relationships, I tell myself to calm the anguish in my chest. Do not try to justify anything because the truth of the facts exists: it happened this or that way. Rationalizing is of no use at this time; in the end, what happened will speak for itself—whether you like it or not, the facts will end up screaming like souls in sorrow. Why do I have to think about these things? I reproach myself, but I cannot prevent the episodes of my life hidden in the nervous tangle that is my brain from coming to light. Crossing the distance of the years come the moans of a girl.

It was terrible and, at the same time, a liberation, to stop being that shy, elusive girl who was indifferent to everything that happened outside of her and went unnoticed even by her own mother. I was invisible. I had become accustomed to spending my hours hidden in that small space under a bed where, without being aware, I hid a secret, an unpronounceable confession and that, nevertheless, made me feel ugly and dirty. The words choked me. I could not make myself understood and, without a voice, that confession became entangled in the darkness of my memory. Around that time, I came to believe myself a ghost trapped in silence. Today I would have been diagnosed as autistic: a creature walled inside, without emotions or desires.

One day, I found myself outside that hole where fear had trapped me. Standing in front of me was a new world, huge, resplendent, and full of options. Fate had brought me to New York. I could have become a bitter, depressed woman, yet I chose to be brave. I was not a warrior. I was a helpless and fearful little animal whom the world threw itself on and forced me to use nails and teeth if she wanted to stay alive. One must run a distance, overcome obstacles, and break one's soul to realize that one walks among beasts. And the trusting ones are destined to end up with their skin and souls peeled off and shattered. It is painful to recognize that one is part of the herd of savages and, as such, also possesses the ability to hurt and destroy. These are the rules imposed by society, ethics, religion . . . responsible for filing and extirpating that divine gift, that human aptitude . . . . What aptitude? That innate condition that runs through our veins, pushes us to kill the one who damages us, or that hurts those we love.

As I grew older, I believed that nothing could hurt me anymore, ignoring that, until our very last breath, life will remind us that only life itself decides and holds the reins. The uncertainty that hovered around my mind and tortured my spirit materialized in front of a work of art, fracturing the security I thought I possessed. Art being the most accurate representation of human drama, it redeems or condemns us. On any given day, my sister and I went to visit the Metropolitan Museum. As always, I wanted to visit the room dedicated to the Impressionists, my favorite room.

Even sensing the danger my sister wanted to move me away from, I insisted, because in the depths of my soul lived the harmful desire to discover an odious reality.

As if hypnotized, I approached *Thérèse Dreaming*. I had seen this work by Balthus many times. But that day, just like Thérèse in the painting, I felt immobilized, prey to an evil reverie. My sister pulled me by one arm and, as I looked at her, I found grief reflected in her eyes. That look was like feeling struck by lightning; its destructive light broke the darkness in my brain, exposing my soul, still a prisoner of fear. My sister's tender and protective embrace gave me the answer that her lips never dared to pronounce. That damn moment of childhood jumped from a recess of memory. I saw the diabolical figure, I heard the pounding of his hooves as he approached me, I perceived the fetidity of his breath, the perversity flashing in his eyes, and I screamed in horror when I met my . . . the face of the person I trusted most, the person I most admired and loved.

I don't know if it was days or weeks that I had a fever, chills, and nightmares, and only my mother's lies managed to calm me and confuse me— "It was an angel, an angel visited you and his light scared you." That he was an angel, or the devil himself, did not prevent fear from leaving me speechless or from looking for a hiding place so that this horrible thing would not find me again. And there I continued to seek refuge in oblivion—not remembering what, who, or why I had escaped. My sister says that the mind creates fantasies and resorts to forgetting traumatic events to protect our ego and pride. My mind managed to save me from horror at a time when I was helpless. At the same time, it blocked the instincts that alert every living being of danger.

It can be called experience or old age, but I think that only the years manage to give that insight that tells one that one is not wrong, that things are as they are even before having evidence in our hands. I'm not defending myself, nor looking for excuses, when I say that the lack of malice with which I was raised made me unaware of the danger. I didn't know how to decipher the suspicious signs hidden behind a look, behind a smile, or a word. I was blind and deaf. Horrible things happened because of that lack of vision, which is why I left my children unprotected and easy prey for human beasts. The pain is unbearable and, above all, the anger that poisons my soul— when I remember the moments I cannot forgive myself for.

Unconscious or not, in the end, one must respond with one's whole life for these oversights. My whole life, my soul will be tormented—my whole life, my mind and my heart will burn with rage and revenge. It was my obligation as a mother to be alert, protect, and defend my children even at the risk of losing my life. Happily, my daughter, at her young age, already owned a refined and wild sixth sense. She sniffed danger from afar, and sounded the alarm. Only then did I open my eyes, look around and see the evil, the cruelty, the hatred that nestled in the dark background of the human soul.

I will never settle for spitting and cursing those beasts; my life will be over, but not the desire to strangle them with my own hands, to burn them. Among the shadows that roam in my brain a shape appears. Love makes my soul shiver when I discover my son's face. I thank life for having enjoyed, for the time it lasted, the gift of the gods that were his tenderness, his admiration, and his trust. I was an idol for that boy; however, as the magic of childhood and adolescence disappeared, he discovered that his mother was not the person he had idealized. He had to endure my temper, my failures, my insecurities, my selfishness . . . . He had to endure my traps, my betrayals, and, worst of all, my inability to show my feelings, to give him my love.

"Maybe I still love you, but I dislike you. The word mother does not fit you," my son says. I can see resentment in his eyes and feel excruciating pain that barely allows me to breathe. He was right: I am aware of not having fulfilled that sacred responsibility that is motherhood. I offered my children food, clothes, shelter, and the comforts that were possible, but not my company and my care. Much later I learned that, on several occasions, after leaving school, my son played in the same *arcade* where the members of one of the Colombian cartels gathered, that the bruises he often showed on his face and arms were the result of the blows that his schoolmates gave him because they could not stand that life had given him the intellectual capacity that it had denied them; they did not tolerate the praise to which he was subjected by his teachers. How many more ugly things did he have to go through? How many times was he in danger? How many things did I not know about my children because I wasn't present in their lives?

One day, my son said he didn't want to see me anymore. Perhaps he thought that this way he would avoid hearing about my latest regrets or that I was a bad influence on his two daughters. If only we could just erase what tortures us, the mistakes of the past. But life gives us only one chance. I know that I loved those two children with all my heart. However, my time and attention were devoted to other things that I considered important then.

I hear that I have only been in the hospital for a day; however, I feel like having slept for days, maybe months. They say I suffered a transient ischemic attack: a blood vessel carrying blood to the brain was clogged, and the affected nerve cells did not receive the necessary amount of oxygen. That is what the doctor explains to my daughter and son-in-law when the truth is that I collapsed, I fell apart under the weight of years of disappointments, anguish, of unreasonable fears. I don't remember doing anything without doubt or anxiety guiding my steps. Just as my brain fails its sense of direction, so was my walk-through life, always hesitant, stumbling, without the certainty of knowing if I was doing the right thing.

Balzac was right to say that I was a "successful failure," because if, after so many defeats and misfortunes, the results favored me, it was not because I planned them or did what I should have done, but because the opportunities given were all in my favor. Many times, I heard about the relationship between cause and effect to explain the behavior of animals and humans. According to this law, to survive, both men and animals learn from their mistakes and save that information for use in similar circumstances. Sheer nonsense! Cause and effect are not sufficient to explain the nature of men. Nor does any purpose determine their behavior because the consciousness of the human being does not follow patterns—it is not a mechanism that obeys mathematical formulas. If not, to what effect was devoting years of my youth to the study of mechanical systems and the functioning of things when such knowledge had no place in the biochemical disorder of my brain? What was the purpose of running like a crazy chicken in marches and protests defending rights and ideals that I didn't give a shit about? I offered my body to men I didn't even want or wasn't interested in; I did it just because I was a female, to have fun for a while. If anyone felt used or was injured, it was not my fault, or even me! Simply, in matters of passion, when something is at stake, anyone can lose. There is no denying that one gains knowledge and experience, but what good is it all if life still continues and nothing guarantees we will live free from bad things?

Sometimes I try to imagine what the world would have been like if I had acted differently, and I can't give it a precise shape. What could I have changed to alter the outcome into something better? I don't think I would be any happier or more miserable in a different world. My sister tells me that if I hadn't come to the United States, I would be someone else. What kind of person? "You would never have developed the guts to challenge the world, become a strong creature, with greater chances to survive and emerge triumphant."

Of course, having lived in New York, the infinite realm of opportunities, offered certain advantages, but the options were given anywhere. The game was to know how to take advantage of them. My sister's words caused me grief and anger. They made me understand that, like others, she thought I was devoid of skills and that my achievement was governed by good luck. "I don't understand," I said, "if I hadn't made it to New York, then I would now be an ape?"

I had to fight to survive. I got bullshit from rude people without a shred of knowledge about me and, much less, empathy, who believed they had the right to crush the newcomers. I was a woman "for factories." I had to live in a swamp in which I had to scratch and claw constantly to prevent the mud from swallowing me. My circumstances marked my character. I learned to be realistic, pragmatic, and nihilistic. Outside of "every man for himself," there was nothing. I admit that I was lucky to accomplish things that I hadn't even known I had in me. Life is like that: you fight for something and get nothing. However, sometimes you get something just because. I know that my attitude is somewhat fatalistic in saying that we should expect both joy and pain, that things will happen whether we want them to or not. The world is as it is, and we cannot change it. I feel chills remembering my arrival in New York. Through the window glass of the plane, I saw this city shining at night and thought that, behind the thousand lights that outshined the brightness of the stars, there was something hidden, unknown, that called out my name, "Elina, Elina, you've arrived, I am waiting for you."

Long after, when everything and everyone failed me: friends, men, religion, eternity, God . . . I saw with sadness that everyone was on the other shore, each with his or her way of being, of seeing, of feeling, each one in their own world, on that other shore, too difficult to reach. When I thought I had lost everything and was alone with myself, I was able to look back and come face to face with that thing that lurked, unknown and hidden then, which appeared to be waiting for my arrival.

It was life. It was the world. It was destiny. In the recollection of certain things that happened, I live them again and shudder.

It was eleven o'clock one night, leaving my job at "the factory," and I was walking completely alone on a Brooklyn Street, next to the Manhattan Bridge, to take the train on York Street, when I saw two guys get out of a car, pull a gagged man out from the back seats, his hands and feet tied up, and throw him into the waters of the East River. I sweated blood when one of the thugs lit up the surroundings with a flashlight. I didn't know if the shadows of the night managed to erase me, but he did not see me. I remember seeing the body of that man swept away by the current and I felt my soul jump, rejoicing. Thus, imagining the remains of what was Carlos Calvo in life had to be lost in the waters.

"El paisa Ospina," one of my homeless Colombian friends, took me with him to see "The Boss," Evelio Romero, so that we could meet. "The friends of my *parces* are my friends," said the Colombian drug lord, known for doing favors and bringing gifts to the people of the neighborhood in exchange for respect and discretion. In that restaurant, *Tierras Colombianas,* I asked Romero for a favor: to cut off the hands and testicles of Carlos Calvo, the scumbag who'd tried to abuse my daughter. I also asked him to put Jovanka Tejada in a box, for a week, without bread or water. Jovanka was the nanny who had left my son, a two-and-a-half-year-old, locked in a closet for eight hours. "The Boss" took notes, nodded, and, with a smile, promised not only to fulfill my request, but to make the woman rot in life, and he assured me that the East River would swallow Carlos Calvo.

Five weeks later, the DEA put several cartel members behind bars, including Evelio Romero. Perhaps it's all part of my vivid imagination or, indeed, the capo had found the time before his capture to fulfill my requests because, from a former neighbor, I later learned that the police had rescued a semi-conscious woman who had been locked up in a garbage container. I heard, also, on the local news, that the decomposed body of an unidentified man whose hands and testicles had been severed was found floating on the waters of the East River.

I feel relief in my chest. I would have felt better if the righteous hands had been mine. I lose consciousness for a moment, but the voices of the past return, and the memories reoccupy my mind. It is with joy that I remember that afternoon when my second husband was about to become a eunuch. I left the house, I went out into the street to make sure my daughter's complaints about his malicious behavior were true. Indeed, my husband was waiting for her in the car to take her to school when he was supposedly at work. I pretended I hadn't seen him, so he wouldn't feel discovered, and headed to the store that was around the corner. I waited until Saturday afternoon when my children went to the movies to claim my justice. I thought I would do it following the plot of a story I had written a few months earlier. In the story, the protagonist kept under her pillow the knife with which she planned to kill her lover. She would do so during orgasm when the man weakened and closed his eyes. I kept the knife on the night table, covered by a scarf—not to kill him, but as a precaution.

Enticingly, I offered him a scotch on the rocks, his favorite drink. He had a couple of drinks, placed the glass on the bedside table, and lay on the bed waiting for pleasure. I pounced on him, removed his clothes and his underwear, and then kissed his belly and looked for his sex. He stroked my hair, enjoying that I stroked his member as I pleased. I will never forget the cry of pain that escaped from his mouth when he felt my teeth dig deep into his cock.

"Fucking bitch!" Unable to get out of the pressure of my teeth, he yanked my hair hard. I wanted to split his penis with my teeth, but the taste of blood in my mouth made me gag and I let go. I jumped up to get the knife. The man, cursing and crying, held his injured phallus.

"Motherfucker, you should thank me that I didn't bite it off," I shouted, unhinged, knife in hand. "This is how you learn about respect! You thought you could touch my daughter and get away with it? Really?! Now, I'm going out shopping and, when I come back, I don't want to find you here. Get out and never come back!"

He looked at me with hatred. "Crazy piece of shit, I should have left you in the asylum forever!"

Before leaving the room, still with the knife raised, I warned him, "If you want, you can report me to the police or whoever you want to, but beware. You know I *am* crazy!"

Several episodes of my life cross my mind as if parts of a film that rewinds and suddenly stops. I feel the stream of frozen water whipping my naked body again. I fall back on the floor because of the violent force of the water. I howl and tremble, not because of the freezing water but from helplessness. It was my fanciful mind and rapturous behavior that caused me to go to the asylum. I found myself cornered behind the bars of a cell like an abandoned dog. I could not complain, let alone scream. If I did, I ran the risk of being immobilized by a straitjacket, receiving electric shocks, or taking a cocktail of pills that would transform me into a zombie.

I futilely try not to think, but the memories insist on torturing me. I cannot remedy it; I feel the tears slip away from me as I reminisce about all these depressing moments:

I run several blocks, my strength abandons me, but I must keep running. At that time of the afternoon, the streets of

Morgan Avenue in Brooklyn are lonely, and no one can help me. At four o'clock in the afternoon, when my shift begins, everyone is busy with their work, swallowing their souls, with rotten lungs, broken backs, and hands in living pain, inside those buildings turned into textile, metallurgical, and chemical sewers. Thousands of factories that pollute the New York of the seventies and eighties, fulfilling the relentless and depressing violence of capitalism of the late twentieth century. I keep running. I cannot let that scumbag chasing me reach me, rape me, kill me, butcher me. I will not end up being one more figure in a police record, another undocumented immigrant girl murdered and sexually abused on the streets of New York.

The door to the factory opens, the supervisor comes out, a huge black woman. I can't take it anymore. I fall, fainting, on the ground. When I wake up, I am lying on one of the tables in the cafeteria as two workers each wave a piece of cardboard on my face. From them, I learn that when the supervisor went out to smoke a cigarette, she found that the rapist had already pulled down my pants.

My body hurts, I think I have too much accumulated fatigue, but I will not let myself be overcome by exhaustion or anything. I decide I must keep running, the asshole will never catch up with me. I run, I keep running. The weight of the little girl I am carrying in my belly doesn't stop me as I run down the stairs to the subway. The immigration officer cannot reach me, he loses sight of me when he runs into hundreds of people waiting for the train and, among them, dozens of Hispanic women who, to him, all look the same. Chance got in his way, my destiny was stronger than his obligation to stop and deport me.

My memories stop. I hear the doctor's voice give Gilly instructions, "Very soon, you can take your mother home. I recommend rest, tranquility, avoid things that alter her. She would like to spend hours by the sea, breathe fresh air, and see nature."

I feel like laughing out loud. Does that deluded man think I'll follow his shitty advice and die watching sand, waves that come and go, and throw bread at the seagulls? That guy, my daughter, and my son-in-law, don't know that as soon as I regain my strength, I'll buy a ticket and go back to New York. If I must die, let it be doing what I want!

"Mom, wake up, open your eyes," my daughter whispers in my ear, caressing my hair. I open my eyes lazily. I had forgotten that light was part of this reality and blink at its brightness.

I find Gilly by my side and my son-in-law sitting at my feet. My eyes comb the room in search of Adrian. I think, "I love you, Adrian."

"Mom, what a joy to see you recovered. You don't know how afraid I was of losing you. Mom, I love you," Gilly says, kissing my forehead.

"I love you, Gilly," I say, smiling. I take her hand. I bring it to my chest. "Where is Adrian?" I ask, despite knowing that my son will not arrive, will not even call me. I didn't know how to be a good mother, in spite of loving my children above all things. I feel like grief shatters my heart, but I won't cry. I won't cry. Oh life! Why so much pain? Why? I've had moments of bliss and dreadful moments; I've known evil and goodness, cowardice and bravery, glory and hell. What was the reason for all this drama that is life? Perhaps it all comes down to knowing that one is alive. It is our passions burning in our body and soul that encourage us. Those passions define us and allow us to understand who we are.

Who are you? I ask myself.

I am Elina, I answer myself.

I am alive, and I know that the pain of this knowledge is the price I pay myself for being who I am.

I must clarify that this novel entitled *Things I cannot say* belongs to the world of fiction. I am sorry to disappoint those readers who came to think that the Elina Cano in the novel and the author are the same person, or that the characters named here are real. They are not. I also clarify that most of the events narrated in the novel are a product of my imagination.

The first chapter tells the experience of the character Vallejo as a witness to the terrorist attack on the towers of the World Trade Center on September 11, 2001. That part is a true story taken from the book *El hombre de Sagitario,* with permission from its author, Ángel García.

ABOUT THE AUTHOR

Elssie Cano, an Ecuadorian writer and author, has lived in the United States since 1970. She has a degree in Mechanical Engineering from the City College of New York and a Masters in Bilingual Education from Universidad Autónoma de Santo Domingo, Dominican Republic. In 2020 Elssie earned a Creative Writing-Fiction-M.F.A. scholarship from New York University (NYU) Graduate School of Arts&Science. She has published *La otra orilla y otros relatos* (Short story, Editorial Surco, 2000), *Fiptisio'89* is its translation to English (Books&Smith New York Editors, 2020), *Mi maravilloso mundo de porquería* (Novel, 2014, winner of the Primum Fictum Award from Librooks Publishing House in Barcelona, Spain), *IDROVUS* (Novel, artepoética Press, 2018), and *Creando a Eva* (Novel, artepoética Press, 2020). She has co-edited *Residencia en Nueva York/Cuentistas Hispanos en (de) Nueva York* (Anthology, artepoética Press, 2021).

Elssie is a member of the editorial staff for the magazine *Hybrido Cultural Project for Latino Arts, Literature and Cultures.*

INDEX

Things I Cannot Say

Nueva York Poetry Press®

INCENDIARY
Fiction Collection
(Homage to Beatriz Guido)

1

Alyz en New York Land
Novel
Jesús Bottaro

2

Historia de una imaginación memorable
Novela
Andrés Felipe López López

3

Things I Cannot Say
Novel
Elssie Cano

SOUTH
Essay Collection
(Homenaje a Victoria Ocampo)

1

quien tropieza por fuera
Miguel Ángel Zapata

BREAK UP
Other discourses
(Homage a to Sylvia Molloy

1

Cáncer de mama: no de alma
Autobiografía
Marta Eugenia Santamaría Marín

POETRY
COLECTIONS

NUEVA YORK POETRY PRESS
INTERNACIONAL POETRY AWARDS

CUARTEL
Award Winning Authors
(Homenage to Clemencia Tariffa)

VIVO FUEGO
Essential Poetry
(Homenage to Concha Urquiza)

PIEDRA DE LA LOCURA
Personal Anthologies
(Homenage to Alejandra Pizarnik)

MUSEO SALVAJE
Latinamerican Poetry
(Homenage to Olga Orozco)

PARED CONTIGUA
Spaniard Poetry
(Homenage to María Victoria Atencia)

CRUZANDO EL AGUA
Poetry in Translation (English to Spanish)
(Homenage to Sylvia Plath)

TRÁNSITO DE FUEGO
Central American and Mexican Poetry
(Homenage to Eunice Odio)

VÍSPERA DEL SUEÑO
Hispanic American Diaspora Poetry
(Homenage to Aida Cartagena Portalatín)

MUNDO DEL REVÉS
Children's Poetry
(Homenage to María Elena Walsh)

LABIOS EN LLAMAS
Opera prima
(Homenage to Lydia Dávila)

MEMORIA DE LA FIEBRE
Poesía feminista
(Homenage to Carilda Oliver Labra)

VEINTE SURCOS
Antologías colectivas
(Homenage to Julia de Burgos)

For those who think like Albert Camus that "thinking is, above all, wanting to create a world (or imitating one's own, which is equivalent to the same)" this book was completed in April 2023 in the United States of America.

www.ingramcontent.com/pod-product-compliance
Lightning Source LLC
Chambersburg PA
CBHW020419030726
47495CB00006B/1574